HOMICIDE ON ROUTE 66

Roger L. Fields

ISBN (Paperback): 979-8-9891177-9-6
ISBN (eBook): 979-8-9891177-6-5

To family and friends
who continuously encouraged me on this journey.

I have always admired and respected the achievements
of William Penn Adair Rogers, a fellow Oklahoman and
Cherokee Nation citizen. Although I chose to use the name
Will Rogers for the main character of this story, this is a
work of fiction and is not intended to depict any events
from the life of William Penn Adair Rogers.

Cover design by Raney Day Creative, LLC.

CHAPTER ONE

It was a typical late-July evening in Northeast Oklahoma, during that time of year when the lack of rain dried the prairie grasses and the air carried the faint aroma of dust and dying wildflowers. Northbound on US Highway 66, I had just passed Longhorn Ranch, an old Route 66 roadside attraction. Saddened by how the years had been so unkind to such an attraction, I recalled times in the past when my family had visited and spent leisure time walking between pens and observing the longhorn cattle, buffalo, and rare livestock on display. Longhorn Ranch was built sometime around 1950. Now, sixty years later, what was left of the original structures had become quite run-down and in disrepair. It seemed folks in the modern era did not have an appetite for roadside attractions that had once been so popular.

As a slight bend in the road gave way to a long straight section, I let my foot relax and my old blue Impala convertible slowed to a comfortable, relaxed speed. I had lowered the top and was enjoying the warm summer air as day began its transition to night. Glancing to the west, I smiled at the beauty of the pastel-purple and orange sky as darkness drifted toward the horizon when I noticed a small gray or light-blue sedan pulled mostly off the roadway on the right shoulder. The last of the evening sun's light shining on the vehicle made the color indistinguishable. Since the vehicle was not quite clear of the road, I slowed to near ten or fifteen miles per hour and eased into the southbound lane. A man dressed in denim pants and a faded red T-shirt standing behind the vehicle looked at me as I slowly rolled past him. His face immediately captured my attention. His skin was dark, with deep wrinkles from the corners of his eyes and down his cheeks. A long deep scar ran from the left corner of his mouth up toward his temple. His face indicated he had led a hard life. Our eyes made contact as we both stared at the other, his eyes dark and bloodshot. While his face testified to his hard life, his eyes invoked feelings of pure meanness. Our brief eye contact caused an uncomfortable feeling in me.

As I passed, I smelled a faint gasoline odor. Perhaps he had been pouring fuel into his vehicle from a gas can and spilled enough to cause the odor. The vehicle was just north of Farm Road 71, where years before I would have turned to the east to visit Jenni, a girl I dated through high school and for a while during college. As I drove away, I felt a hint of guilt. Normally, I would stop to see if a stranded motorist needed help, but for some reason, stopping had not even crossed my mind.

The remaining fifteen minutes of my drive were uneventful but a bit uncomfortable. I occasionally thought back to the face of the man at the side of the road. I do not think it was fear but discomfort I felt each time I saw that image in my mind. It surprised me how many memories I had from my travels up and down that road, like the time I ran out of gas in a friend's 1962 Ford truck and walked to a farmhouse to call a friend to bring some gas.

Just as the sun set and the air began to cool, I arrived at Josh and Amy's house. Josh and I had been best friends since third grade and had been the best man at each other's wedding. His wife, Amy, was small but big at heart. She was a quiet, calm soul but quick with a strong word if someone was out of line. She had comforted me through several difficult times over the past twenty years. Amy and Jenni had been the only things to get me through losing my parents the summer after I graduated high school. Next to Jenni and my first wife, Amy was the love of my life. Without her, I never would have believed a man and a woman could have such a strong emotional bond and not be romantically involved.

As usual for that time of year, we sat at their outdoor table for dinner. The table and all but one chair were a steel-mesh pattern that became cool after the sun had set. The outdoor furniture was a gift from their children a couple of years before. As we enjoyed our dinner, we sat and talked about various activities from the day and their teenage son. He had run a red light and hit another vehicle. The damage was slight and nobody had been injured, but his actions had created great drama for the family. In the background, I could hear a television just inside the kitchen. Typically, when we sat outside for dinner, we would turn on the television so we could watch from outside. It always added good background noise that helped break the occasional silence in our conversations.

As we sat and talked, the cushion in my chair had shifted and the mesh design had left an impression on the back of my leg. While adjusting my cushion, I shifted myself in the chair and glanced toward the television. A breaking news story caught my eye. I rose from my chair and walked toward the kitchen. Channel 8 was broadcasting live from the site of an apparent homicide, showing an image of excitement and what appeared to be confusion. The red and blue lights swept their colors across the tall, dry prairie grass in the background as the young lady reporter, posed in front of the camera, struggled to secure a detailed statement from Carlin County Sheriff Joe Robertson. A homicide was a rare occurrence in this area, and the lack of experience was visible from all involved.

After several minutes of live coverage, in order to provide an update for viewers who had just joined, the reporter announced the initial details of the story. She said they were broadcasting live from the scene of an apparent homicide on Route 66, near Farm Road 71, and then continued her update. Authorities were unable to determine whether the victim was male or female. The sheriff had commented that, due to the condition of the body, the Oklahoma State Bureau of Investigation would be called upon for their resources to identify a burn victim. The sheriff had disclosed that they believed it was a homicide, suspecting that gasoline had been used as an accelerant. He stated a clear gasoline odor was present.

As I listened to the broadcast, I could see the image of the man standing behind the vehicle. I could see him as clearly as I saw Josh and Amy sitting in front of me. Up to that point in the evening, I had not mentioned my drive from home, nor the man alongside the road, to Josh and Amy. It didn't warrant discussion, or so I thought.

Josh, Amy, and I were gathered around the television, anxiously awaiting details of the event. Amy, in frustration, remarked, "I wish they would give us more information, and let us know what is going on."

That is when I broke my silence. I walked them through every detail. I described the man's face but found myself incapable of providing a description that accurately characterized his aged, scarred face and the sense of evil I got from his eyes. They sat stunned. It took a few minutes for them to even respond. But they started asking questions.

"Was the man young or old?"

"What color was the car?"

"What kind of car was it?"

"Do you think he did it?"

When they finally paused, I supplied answers. Amy, in a reluctant, hopeful tone, said, "William Lee Rogers, you are lying to us."

I said, "No, 'Mom,' I am not lying to you." In my entire life, only two people, in times of anger or anxiousness, called me by my full given name—my mom and Amy. Even when Amy was angry at me, addressing her as "Mom" typically broke the tension and brought smiles and laughter. Any other time, she used my preferred name, Will.

The entire event, albeit brief, was so vivid and clear in my mind. I answered their questions with specific, descriptive details. Finally, with an expression I had never seen from him, Josh turned and advised, "You must go to the sheriff's office and tell them everything you saw." Amy agreed.

I turned toward them, hesitated, and then replied. "You both know my family and our history with the sheriff's office. You know we are not folks who voluntarily walk through those doors."

This discussion continued for the rest of the evening as we watched occasional news updates. I knew their suggestion was the right thing to do but had always believed there were times to get involved and times not to get involved.

At the end of the evening, the thirty-minute drive home was different that night. My mind was so preoccupied with the images and the fact that someone had lost their life. Knowing I possibly had details that could help identify a murderer weighed heavily on me. "We do not get involved," I kept telling myself. Even though I decided to follow a different route home, all the images in my mind were of that short section of Route 66.

Even after being in bed for some time, I could not stop the images from replaying over and over in my mind, from the times when our eyes made contact, I smelled the gasoline and gazed at the car, and I heard Josh saying, "You must go to the sheriff's office and tell them everything you saw." It was a video loop I could not stop.

I had some hope that I might at least get a brief sleep and awaken to a new day, possibly with some relief from the constant reflections of that evening. After tossing and turning for hours, I did manage a bit of sleep. There did seem to be some relief the next morning as I made my coffee and prepared breakfast. I had been raised on a farm, where we started each day with a full, hearty breakfast, and today would be no different. I am a man of routine, and going through the motions of my daily routine was providing some relief from the constant thoughts of the previous evening. But as I made my way to the barn to warm up my old Ford tractor, the thoughts came flooding back—that same video loop playing over and over.

I had been working to beat the rain forecasted for midweek and needed to finish cutting the last twenty or so acres of bottomland. Rain on the cut grass would spoil the hay and render it useless. This cutting was not a make-or-break issue for me, but it would be good to have in an emergency or if a neighbor ran short that winter. Working through the morning, I did manage to cut several acres but had maintained a constant eye on my watch, to ensure I stopped before noon for lunch.

My normal routine was to watch the noon news and catch the daily ag report as I made myself a sandwich and sat for a few minutes to relax and take a break from the morning's labor. There would not be much relaxation that day, as I was even a bit more anxious to watch and listen, hoping for any additional details from the previous evening. No surprise, the homicide was the leading news story for the day. Channel 8 was broadcasting live from the county courthouse. Since they'd had some time to investigate and prepare statements, things appeared much more organized than the live events from the previous coverage. It was an uncommon display for our small courthouse to have media from around the state shoving microphones in the sheriff's direction as he began his remarks. Most of the statement repeated the information provided from live coverage at the scene, but some new details were made available, including that the victim was confirmed to be a female, though it would be several weeks before they might make a positive identification.

I literally yelled out loud, "Oh, God, how have I not thought about Jenni?"

Chapter Two

Jenni and I dated through high school and for most of my first year in college. I graduated high school in 1988. Jenni graduated in 1990. A couple of years after Jenni and I had broken up, she and Russell Robertson had a brief whirlwind romance and engagement and were quickly married in a small, private ceremony. Unfortunately, and surprising to all of us, Russell turned out to be very abusive toward Jenni. During a chance encounter at the local grocery store, Jenni's mother told me about Russell's abuse. She wept as she talked about the marks and bruises Jenni had shown her, beginning shortly after her and Russell's wedding. Ultimately, that issue started a rift between the sheriff and me. I had tried for the past few years not to involve myself in Jenni's private life, but her fear and inability to walk away from an abusive relationship left me feeling that I must get involved. A person with her kind heart and loving demeanor should never suffer at the hands of an abusive spouse. Fortunately, Russell and Jenni did not have any children during their years of marriage.

I discussed the abuse with the sheriff on more than one occasion but was unable to move him to action. In rural Oklahoma, most folks realize that becoming sheriff is virtually a lifetime appointment, and blood is thicker than statutes. We had always referred to the sheriff as "Sheriff Joe." Joe Robertson was his name, but when he initially took office, he let it be known that he preferred to be called Sheriff Joe. I always assumed he thought that would make him more personable. Russell was Sheriff Joe's nephew and had been living on the wrong side of right and wrong for a long time. He understood his protection from law enforcement and took advantage at every turn. Things became very tense between Sheriff Joe and me as I continued to push for him to intervene in Jenni's situation. I had openly campaigned for his opponent in the last couple of elections, but it was virtually impossible to unseat a sheriff once he had taken office. I had always believed that any elected official who did not execute their responsibilities evenly and fairly should not hold public office. But I also realized the puzzle that was small-town politics was no different than big-city politics—it was just easier to see all the pieces.

It only took one mistake by Russell for Jenni to force him out of her life for good. One evening while they were having dinner at the Main Street Café in town, Russell erupted into one of his irrational tirades and slapped Jenni. Someone in the restaurant called the city police, who promptly arrested Russell. I was certain that Sheriff Joe's protection did not extend to the local police department. Jenni's family and I convinced her to use that opportunity to press charges on Russell and file for a long-overdue divorce.

It was several years later that Jenni met her second husband, Scott Barro. A short time before Jenni and Scott's wedding, as I walked the aisles of the local Walmart, I ran into Scott and Jenni and had a brief conversation. As we chatted, I saw she was still as beautiful as when we had dated. After a few minutes, as we began to walk away, Jenni asked, "Will, do you still mess with old CB radios?"

I turned and said with a smile, "I have not messed with them in years but would love to again if I had the chance. Y'all take care."

When we dated in high school, Jenni and I had a very secluded place at the lake where we would escape from the world and love away the hours. It was not far from the farm where Jenni had been raised. We called our special place "Cain's Bayou." Neither of us had actually been to a bayou in our lifetime, but we agreed it must be what a bayou looked like. The name "Cain's" came from an old Cain's Coffee can we'd found the first time we visited that wonderful place. For the remaining years of our relationship, we had a simple code to tell each other we wanted to meet. We would find a way to use the acronym "CB" in a sentence. Or, on occasion, one of us would call the other

Charlie Brown and a date was set. It was our fun, covert way of telling the other to meet that night at Cain's Bayou.

That conversation at Walmart left me with an inability to focus on anything for the remainder of the day. I asked myself over and over, "Was she telling me she wanted to meet at Cain's Bayou? Or was it just fun flirtation?" I was not even sure the area was still vacant. "Do I dare drive out there?" I continued asking myself the question, but inside I knew that nothing was going to keep me away from Cain's Bayou that night.

CHAPTER THREE

Scott and Jenni were happily married for almost five years, living on Jenni's family farm. Jenni's parents had died some years earlier and left the farm to her. Farming was not a way of life that Scott knew, and he was not the handiest of men around a farm, but he worked hard, and he treated Jenni like a queen. For that, he had my respect.

On their anniversary date three years ago, Scott died unexpectedly and left Jenni with a young son and a daughter. They were so cute and mischievous. James, the oldest, was four at the time. Little Jenni was two and favored her mom in appearance and demeanor. It was easy to see, that even at her young age, she would grow to possess her mom's strength and grace. I enjoyed the brief periods of time I had been around them. Even on bad days, they put a smile on my face. Taking a minute to throw a ball with them, or tell them a story, reminded me of the early times with my own children.

I never expected any rekindled romance between Jenni and me, but I occasionally stopped by her house for a cup of coffee and to check up on her and her children. If she needed small repairs or work done, I would do what I could for her. Like so many folks in rural areas of the country, Scott did not leave behind a life insurance policy to help Jenni manage finances on a farm with an aging barn and farm equipment. Financial strain combined with years of being a single mother can take a toll on a person, but somehow Jenni still had hope for better days and hadn't lost that smile and laugh that made her so attractive to me. Not wanting to create any conflict between them while Scott was still alive, I tried to ensure I maintained some distance. I had been happy for them when I learned of their first child, born within their first year of marriage. I had chuckled at the thought that it did not take Scott long to get that first child.

Now, different thoughts occupied my mind. My heart raced as I realized Jenni and her children lived less than a mile from that horrible scene. I also found that, during a recent change of cellular phones, her number had been one of the many lost during the transfer of my contact information. Without any family in the area, the only way I knew to contact her was to go to her house. I did not stop to change into clean clothes, or even rinse the dust from my face. I grabbed the keys to my farm truck, made sure the barn door was locked, and raced to town. If there was ever a good day for no police on the road, it was that day. I made record time getting to the north side of town. As I made the turn in the road to travel north toward Longhorn Ranch, I grasped the precarious position I was about to put myself into. I braked hard and made an abrupt left turn onto a dirt road headed south. I was still traveling fast enough to create a large, thick cloud of dust. At the first driveway I came to, I turned my truck around, pulled to the side of the road, and stopped. The cloud of dust now slowly blew through the cab of my truck, making me cough and choke. I turned off the ignition and tried to clear the dust and my mind.

I had already decided that Josh's recommendation that I report what I had seen on Route 66 was the right thing to do. A visit to Sheriff Joe's office was inevitable, but I understood that if the victim was Jenni, our relationship and my occasional visits to her farm would put me in a tough position with him, especially when I acknowledged being at that location on Route 66 on that evening. The convenience store located on the south side of the old Longhorn Ranch site would have security cameras that probably showed me driving past that evening, and would also show me returning the next day. If I drove to her house and she was home, everything would be all right. If I drove to her house and deputies from the sheriff's office were there, I could be throwing myself into the middle of a homicide investigation, probably as the prime suspect. But knowing that I was likely on security video at Longhorn Ranch, even if I did not go to Sheriff Joe and provide a statement, he would be knocking on my door regardless. Not sharing what I knew, in Sheriff Joe's eyes, would be incriminating. I decided a visit to Jenni's farm that day may not be a wise idea. I would return another day.

CHAPTER FOUR

Our small county courthouse sat in the middle of the town square. It was old but remained a solid structure, having been built with gray limestone rock quarried and cut into large rectangular blocks. It had survived decades of use and renovations, each update intended to modernize it in structure and functionality. Parking spaces were provided around the perimeter of the property, leaving a bit of a walk to enter the building.

I exited my old farm truck and began the walk to the front door of the courthouse. I stopped to view the names on the "World Wars Monument" located in the middle of the sidewalk. I had read those names many times over the years and knew I was just delaying the impending conversation. I made my way through the front doors and turned down the hallway toward Sheriff Joe's office. Reflecting on previous occasions when I had walked those halls, I became uncomfortable as I looked at the well-worn tile and the walls painted with what I'd always called "government-green paint." I had walked those halls more than a couple of times for personal issues, or those involving close family members.

At last, I arrived at the door with the aged lettering, "Carlin County Sheriff." Like so many old government offices, the upper half of the door was a snowflake-patterned glazed glass designed to make the space not seem so closed in and allow some light to penetrate the door. As I reached for the doorknob, the door sprang open and Sheriff Joe came bolting through, knocking me off balance. As he passed and continued down the hallway, he looked at me and said, "What have you done now?"

I immediately thought this was not going to go well. "I need a few minutes of your time to talk about something I saw a couple of nights ago."

He said, "Make an appointment with Beverly and we will talk when I have time. I am busy."

I turned to walk away but, understanding the importance of my visit stopped and told him, "I need to discuss the murder the other night north of Longhorn Ranch."

I had his attention. He stopped, turned, walked toward me, and asked, "What did you do, Will?"

I asked him, "Do you have time to go into your office and speak? I do not want to discuss it openly in the hallway of the courthouse."

As we entered his office, I was immediately struck by its appearance. He had some personal effects, family pictures, personal mementos, and a couple hunting photos, but outside of that, only well-worn government-issued office equipment occupied the space. The desk and file cabinet appeared to be World War II–era issue. I thought to myself, "I wonder how many people have occupied this office since this stuff was brought in here."

He got to the point and promptly asked what I had for him. I walked him through the story from the point where I turned north onto Route 66 at Longhorn Ranch. The video played in my mind as I described every detail. I provided a thorough description of the man, including his dark leathery skin and his deep scar. I had not told the story since sharing it with Josh and Amy and was surprised at how it stayed exactly as I had told them. He sat in silence until I had shared every detail. He yelled through his half-open door, "Beverly, get the DA in here now. And do not let him tell you he is busy." He looked at me and said, "This is how this is going to go. You are going to repeat everything you just told me for the district attorney. We are going to record your statement. And we will bring in a sketch artist. Do you think you can work with them to create a sketch of the man you saw?"

"I can try."

Beverly yelled from the outer room, "The DA will be down shortly."

While we sat waiting for the district attorney to arrive, I asked, "Has anybody gone by to check on Jenni Whittington and her children?" Sheriff Joe ignored my inquiry, but I repeated my question with an obvious frustration in my voice. "Has anybody gone by to check on Jenni Whittington and her children?"

This time, he gave the reply I half expected. "I am not going to discuss any details of this case with you."

I chuckled aloud at the absurdity of that statement. With a few minutes of uncomfortable silence ahead of me, I reflected on the time when Sheriff Joe was still a deputy and visited me at a friend's house.

I had been visiting when my friend and I heard a knock on the door. As my friend opened the door, the deputy asked if I was there. My friend said yes, and the deputy asked if I would come outside to talk. When I went outside, we shook hands and I asked him what he needed. He'd replied, "You are not in any trouble. I just want to tell you not to go on the twenty acres of timber on the north side of your place. Someone is growing marijuana up there. We know it is not you but need you to stay away regardless. We'll let you know when it is safe to go back up there."

I thought back on how time and events can change relationships. We had gone from a cooperative and friendly relationship to the current antagonistic bitterness of today.

Not surprising to me, the conversation with the district attorney was even more awkward than with the sheriff. The discussion went much like the one with Sheriff Joe earlier. It was extremely businesslike. Like the sheriff, the district attorney asked whether I recognized the man.

"I did not recognize him, but I will never forget that face," I said.

They recorded the entire session and asked many questions, which I answered honestly, but briefly. The sketch artist they had intended to use was unavailable. So they decided to try again at another time. As I rose from my chair, Sheriff Joe handed me a business card and told me, "If you think of anything else, give me a call."

My time with the sheriff and the district attorney left me with a heartbreaking feeling about Jenni. At the conclusion of the interview, as I was walking past Beverly's desk, I turned, looked at Sheriff Joe, and asked, "Would there be any issue if I stopped by for a visit with Jenni? As you know, she lives close to that horrible scene. I would like to go by and check on her and her kids."

He said, "I would stay away from the Whittington place."

As I drove away from the courthouse square and considered my current position with the sheriff's department, I realized he knew virtually everything I could tell him related to that evening and Jenni Whittington. Whether or not he warned me to stay away from her home, that was not going to change, and neither was my story. So when I arrived at the junction in the road to choose between turning toward the farm or going into town, I continued toward town. After making a brief stop and taking a minute to add some oil to my old farm truck, I was on my way to Jenni's.

I turned onto the dirt road to Jenni's place and reflected on the many times I had made that nearly one-mile journey from the highway, anxious to pick her up and spend the night laughing and enjoying time with her. Times had not always been smooth. We shared times that were tense and painful. Thinking that Jenni may be gone made memories of the painful times seem less painful. Those were the youthful experiences that taught us about relationships, the give and take required. Although I had traveled that short journey several times over the past few years, I saw things differently this time. I saw fences falling down, trees overgrown in the fence rows, and pastures not mowed. The tension escalated and my fear of what I may soon discover had my heart racing.

As I pulled my old truck into the driveway, the knot in my stomach tightened. Neither Jenni nor the kids came out the door to welcome me. It was eerily quiet, and I was hesitant to approach the house. The only things to be heard were the sounds of cars and trucks traveling the interstate highway in the distance and the wind blowing through two large oak trees in the front yard. Lobo, the family dog, an Australian shepherd and Labrador mix, slowly trotted from the barn toward me. I called his name and asked, "Where is everybody, old boy?" He escorted me to the door as I knocked, hoping to hear a voice or see the door swing open. Neither of those things happened regardless of how many times I knocked. I walked around the circumference of the house, looking for signs of anybody. I walked through the barn hoping for someone to appear and say, "I did not hear you drive up." But nobody cried out a welcome. Jenni's Chevy sedan was in the driveway and her truck was in the barn, so I received no comfort of thinking they had simply run to town.

After a couple of minutes of searching, I located Lobo's dog food, filled his water and food bowls, and sat on an old lawn chair outside the barn. From the way Lobo went after the fresh food in his bowl, it was clear he had probably not eaten in a day or two, another sign that things were not right. Jenni's children were normal kids, running and playing without a care in the world, but they loved their dog and always made sure he was watered and fed.

There was a decent breeze blowing, and it was still comfortable sitting in the shade of the barn. Lobo finished his breakfast and lay down beside me. He appeared to appreciate and enjoy having a visitor. After thirty to forty minutes sitting with him, I knew it was time to get back to the farm and make some progress at getting hay baled and into the barn. But when I rose to leave, I told myself, "Just a few more minutes. Maybe they will come home." I tried to leave numerous times but could not. Twice, I walked around the house, the well house, and the barn and returned to my chair, moving it occasionally to maintain my protection from the heat of the late-July sun. Eventually, I moved my chair to the shade of one of the oak trees. From that vantage point, I sat and stared at Jenni's old barn, remembering the solid, red structure it had been when we dated. Now the paint was faint and the doors were askew or missing altogether. I asked myself, "Why have you not spent more time helping her take care of this place?"

After a couple of hours, I looked at Lobo and said, "Hey, old boy, I do not think they are coming home." But I struggled to make myself leave. I think leaving meant accepting the most painful of possible scenarios. I was not ready to acknowledge that.

I made my way to my truck to find a piece of paper and an ink pen to scratch out a note for Jenni.

Jenni, I dropped by to check on you and the kids. Waited a while, but nobody showed. Lobo's food and water bowls were empty, so I took him home with me. I will return him when you get home. Please call me. Charlie Brown

Knowing that Jenni used the back door primarily, I taped the note there and began the sorrowful walk to my truck.

Lobo was not at all hesitant to jump in the seat of my old truck, and ready to go for a ride. I stopped at the grocery store to pick up a few things and buy some dog food for him. He seemed quite content as we drove along. We had the windows down, and he occasionally held his head out, letting the wind blow across his face. When we arrived home, I took some time to watch him and ensure he did not run away. But he just ran and ran with his nose to the ground. I guess there was a whole world of new scents for him. I hated to tie up a dog but was afraid he may wander away, so I put him on a leash on the porch. I told him that after he had a bath, I would let him stay in the house with me—something Jenni would never dream of doing.

I spent the remainder of the day working in the hayfield. I was beginning to accept what may be one of the most painful outcomes of my life. But if it was Jenni, where were the children? I became so preoccupied with my thoughts of the children and the situation that I ran probably fifteen minutes with no twine in my hay baler. If it was Jenni, what would happen to the children? There were no grandparents, aunts, or uncles to take them in.

CHAPTER FIVE

Lobo and I got along well for a couple of days. On day two, I did manage to get him in the creek with some shampoo. We wrestled for a while, but he eventually succumbed to the inevitable: he was going to get a bath. Probably more accurately stated, we were both going to get a bath. As I cleaned and scrubbed his fur, I told him stories about my brothers and me bathing in that same creek as children. He did not appear to be amused. As we returned to the house, I secured his leash to a post on the front porch to let him dry and keep him from rolling in the dirt and becoming a ball of mud. I told him I would return in a couple of hours and made my way to town and the local Walmart for the weekly grocery run.

As I crossed the parking lot from my truck to the store, I walked past a small light-blue sedan with a Missouri license plate and a trunk decal that read, "Hilltop Used Auto Sales, Salem, MO." I told myself, "That looks like the car," and suddenly realized that when I had seen the man standing behind the car, I could not see the license plate. As I continued my way into the store, I wondered why a car from Salem, Missouri, would be in this part of the country. Salem is a small, quaint town several hours' drive away. My sister and her family had lived there in the early 1990s, and I had visited on a couple of occasions. So I was familiar with that area.

Things were fairly routine for me. My menu did not have a lot of variety; it had consistency. I knew my way through Walmart and the location of the things I purchased every week. The only change to my shopping habit that week was dog food and something for Lobo to chew on. Hopefully, that would keep him from gnawing on my furniture.

I had secured my items and was making my way from the pet foods section to the registers when a man caught my attention. He appeared to be reading the label on some cleaning product. As I walked by him, he began to nod hello, but as our eyes locked, we recognized each other. I was surprised but tried to act as though he was just another shopper. I thought as I walked past that he was about to call out my name.

I quickly made my way to the checkout, placed my items on the conveyor, and asked the cashier to please hurry. She scanned and bagged my items as I stood fidgeting nervously. This time as I walked past the blue sedan, I memorized the tag number and mumbled to myself, "Why do you never have a pen when you need one?" I tossed my groceries in the front seat with the dog food on the floorboard, grabbed a piece of paper and a pen, and recorded the tag number.

As I pulled onto the highway and turned south, I shuffled through my wallet trying to find Sheriff Joe's card he had given me a couple of days before. My hands were shaking as I retrieved it and dialed his number on my cell phone. Just my luck, Beverly answered and advised the sheriff was not in the office. I explained to her that I must speak with him now. The best I could get from her was an uninspiring commitment to have him call me back. I told her, "I must speak with him as soon as possible. I have some information about the homicide on Route 66." I was confident that would get her attention and maybe motivate her to give some effort to getting the sheriff to return my call.

It was only a few minutes later that I received his call. I quickly described passing the man in the store and seeing the car in the parking lot. He asked whether I was certain it was the same man. My response was a quick and confident, "Yes." I supplied the license plate number from the vehicle in the parking lot. He informed me that, without evidence tying the man to the vehicle, it would be a leap to assume it was his vehicle, but he would run the plates. I explained that I believed it was the vehicle I had seen at the side of the road.

I arrived at home and unloaded my groceries. It felt good to have someone or something there to greet me with excitement. Lobo continued running to the end of his leash as he tried to get my attention. As I reflected on my impression that the man was about to call my name, it also felt good that Lobo would be in the house with me. If the man indeed knew my name, it was likely he also knew where I lived. An extra set of ears listening for abnormal activity in the night would be comforting.

That evening, I grilled a couple hamburgers on an old makeshift homemade grill as Lobo lay in the shade, appearing to enjoy the occasional waft of cooking beef carried by the light evening breeze. I had retrieved an old holster for my nine-millimeter pistol and had it on my right hip. Supper and the rest of the evening had gone without incident as I settled into my easy chair to watch television. Shortly after sunset, Lobo sprang to his feet and began barking. As I turned to tell him to be quiet, I noticed headlights coming up the driveway. I immediately hooked the leash to Lobo's collar and secured it to the leg of the sofa. I grabbed my nine-millimeter and raced out the back door, taking cover behind the well house, where I had a vantage point of someone parking and going to my front door. As the car turned and parked, the front porch light lit up the car and I could clearly see the lights on top of it and then the Carlin County Sheriff emblem on the driver-side door. As the sheriff exited his patrol car, I yelled out, "Sheriff Joe, it is me, Will. I am behind the well house, and I am armed. I am coming out with my hands raised."

He yelled, "When you are clear of the well house, turn your back to me and begin walking backward. When I tell you to, stop and slowly lay your weapon on the ground and step away from it."

I complied with his instructions and put some distance between me and my firearm. He retrieved my pistol from the ground and secured it in his patrol car. He holstered his sidearm and asked if we could go inside and talk.

As we entered the living room, Lobo continued to voice his thoughts on having a visitor. I removed him to the porch and returned to learn what was on the sheriff's mind. As I sat in my chair, he looked at me and said, "That dog looks familiar. Is that Jenni Whittington's dog?"

I said, "Yes, it is her dog."

He said, "That means you have been to her place. I told you to stay away from there."

Lobo may have indicated to him that I had been to Jenni's place, but his question told me he had been there as well. That created great concern for me. I asked, "What is the purpose of your visit at this hour?"

"This is something I should not do, and it goes against the most basic protocols, but I am going to share some information with you. We ran the plates on the vehicle you called in. It came back registered to Jake Cummings. I know you and Jake had that incident years ago brandishing handguns on each other, with bad blood for some time after that. That is the only reason I am telling you this."

"The man I saw was not Jake Cummings. I believe the man was about to speak my name as I passed him in the store, but it was not the Jake Cummings I have known since childhood."

The sheriff said, "I ran wants and warrants on Jake and did receive a photo of him. The years in and out of prison have not been kind to Jake, but I assure you, that is Jake."

As he handed me the photo, it only took a glance to recognize the face. I half shouted, "That is the man I saw."

"If that is the scar you saw, I think that makes it an unmistakable identification."

"That is the scar, but that does not look like the Jake Cummings I knew."

I assumed he was not going to answer any questions from me, but I had to determine whether he would share information beyond what he had just provided. I asked him, "Sheriff, was Jenni the homicide victim?"

"We do not have confirmation of the identity, but I will tell you, Jenni is missing. She has not been seen since that night, and we found her children alone in the house."

I immediately replied. "Where are the children now?"

I could see him carefully weighing his answer, but he eventually said, "They are with County Child Protective Services. They are being taken care of."

I asked, "Is it possible for me to see them? I know Jenni had no family and there are probably very few friendly faces that they know. And they know me. It might be good if I could spend some time with them."

His reply was quick and painful, but even I had to under-stand the position of law enforcement and Child Protective

Services. "Until this investigation is complete, or you are cleared of any wrongdoing, you will not be allowed to see the children or even know their location. We know you visited Jenni from time to time over the past few years, and that makes you a person of interest. Not to mention the fact that you admitted to being at the scene that evening."

As he was getting into his patrol car, he again remarked that if I remembered any additional details to give him a call. He removed the clip from my nine-millimeter, cleared the shell in the chamber, and handed them to me through the window as he said, "Keep your eyes open around here. We are looking for him."

I had to acknowledge that, given our past, our visit was fairly cordial, but businesslike. At least we were able to sit and have a discussion without our personal feelings being disruptive.

CHAPTER SIX

It took a few days, but thanks to some help from a neighbor down the road, the hay had been baled, hauled, and neatly stacked in the barn. I was quickly learning about the reality of aging on the human body. Hauling and stacking hay has a way of reminding you just how old you are. It is definitely a young man's activity. But, like a young man, once finished, I enjoyed a visit to the creek to cool myself from the day's labor and wash away the salt that had accumulated and dried on my skin.

I was returning to the house when I saw the sheriff's car coming up the road. Even though our last couple of visits had proven not to be too tense, I could not keep myself from becoming nervous at the sight of his patrol car coming my way. I walked across the yard to greet him as he pulled into the driveway. As he exited his patrol car, I offered a friendly greeting. "Good afternoon, Sheriff Joe. How are you?"

"I am fine, but we need to talk," he said sternly. It was still warm outside, but a breeze was blowing, and the sun was setting behind the hill to the west, providing a relatively comfortable evening. I invited him to the porch and offered him a glass of iced tea or water. He said, "I would appreciate a glass of iced water."

When I returned with two glasses of iced water, we sat and he began to speak.

"You have had your share of minor brushes with the law over the years, and surely understand that we have been checking every detail of your earlier statement. We still consider you a person of interest."

I got it, but hearing the words spoken out loud had an impact on me. "Yes, I have understood that from the beginning."

"Well, understand that you have not been cleared, but we uncovered something that puts me in an extremely difficult position. While searching Jenni's house, we found a letter with your name on it. It was near the top of a stack of mail that had never made it to the mailbox. Since you are a person of interest, we were inclined to open and read it."

Just as I began to ask, "What did it say?" he extended his hand holding the letter.

Nervously, I folded back the flap of the envelope and removed the paper inside. I unfolded the paper and began to read.

Will,

I am not sure why I feel compelled to do this at this time, but nonetheless, I believe it is time to let you know that James is your son. I am sure you have already calculated the months following that night at Cain's Bayou to when James was born. Scott never knew, and I could see no reason to tell him. But I feel I must tell you now.

I am asking for nothing, and expect nothing, but in my heart, I believe it would be unfair to continue to keep this from you. Whether or not you are involved in his life, and how, is a decision that can only be made by you. I will accept whatever you decide. When you have time, it would be best if we discussed your decision so I can decide how best to inform James. He also has a right to know who his father is.

Lastly, I have no regrets about our night at Cain's Bayou. That one night made me feel young, reckless, and free again. And we created a child, the greatest gift we could share.

Let's speak soon,
Jenni

The sheriff gave me a few minutes to collect my thoughts and grasp what I had just read. I reread the letter a few times, paused for a moment, and asked, "Sheriff Joe, after reading this, I must ask again. Is it possible for me to meet with Jenni's children?"

He said, "It appears that Jenni's son is your child, but with Jenni being a missing person, you being a person of interest puts us in a tough situation. I wish I could let you visit with her children, but it would be an unprecedented move. I do not believe you contributed to her disappearance, especially after reading this letter, but until we have completed our investigation of you, I just do not see how we can allow it."

I thought it over for a minute and asked, "What about a supervised visit at Child Protective Services? If it is Jenni, knowing that her children have no family, I will pursue custody later."

He said, "A supervised visit would be your only hope at this point. Regardless, you might contact CPS and start asking what the process of requesting custody would be in the event you are cleared. I will ask about a supervised visit and let you know the decision." With that, he rose from his chair, took one last sip of water, set his glass on the table between the chairs, and walked toward his patrol car.

I escorted him across the yard and thanked him. "I appreciate you letting me know about the letter. It leaves me with a lot of thinking to do."

"I felt it was the right thing to do. I will be in touch." As he backed his patrol car out of the driveway and rolled toward the main road, I began to feel the weight of what I had read.

It was not as if I had spent a lot of time with Jenni and her children after Scott died, but I had been to the house many times. How had I never suspected anything? "I have a seven-year-old son," repeated over and over in my mind. "Am I ready to be a father to a seven-year-old again?" I cried out loud, "Jenni, where are you?"

Every day working on the farm passed at a painfully slow pace as I awaited word from the sheriff or CPS. I maintained my regular routine and pretended everything was the same as it had always been, but so many thoughts poured through my mind, reminding me these times were not routine. Every pause in work had me checking my phone in case noise from the tractor had kept me from hearing a call. Each time brought the same result, no call and no voice message. At least two times per day, I made a trip to the mailbox hoping for written notification from CPS regarding a supervised visit with James and Little Jenni. Each trip left me feeling empty, as there were only mailers and occasional bills. I was hesitant to contact CPS about letting the children stay with me. It seemed logical to me that if I was allowed to visit with them, then that would be the time to initiate the conversation. And I was still clinging to the hope that Jenni would be found.

Josh and Amy had visited multiple times over the past few weeks. Their visits and their ability to keep me calm and rational were the only things that gave me hope and comfort during this difficult time. One warm evening, the three of us were sitting on the porch relaxing and passing the time with some idle chat. While Josh was in the house refilling his drink, I asked Amy, "Do you remember Pastor Bill, the old guy who preached at the Pentecostal church in town when we were kids? When we were teenagers, he told me something I have always remembered. He said, 'Will, clouds last only for a moment, but the sun is always present. It may rain, but the sun is still there. You must have a belief and an expectation that you will see it, even before it shines through, between the clouds. That is called faith.' I'm not sure I understood what he meant until now. But at this time, the only thing I see is clouds. All I have is an expectation. I need to see some light shining soon."

Amy said, "I am certain the light is coming soon, Will."

Three days passed—then four, five, and six. I hoped that day seven would be the day I received some information. Even word of a delay would be welcome. Something. Anything. Just confirmation that some forward movement was happening. I told myself out loud, "The wheels of bureaucracy do turn slowly."

I had spent the morning of day seven in the field, mowing the areas left uncut from harvesting hay. My old tractor chugged along as I made my way through the field working my way back to the barn. This had been a long, slow morning, and I looked forward to lunch. A splash of cold water on my face and my customary sandwich would bring a welcome break in the day. As I approached the barn, I could see a patrol car a quarter mile down the road. Again, I recognized the sheriff's patrol car as he turned onto my road. This time, he did not park in the driveway; he drove through the open gate and straight to the barn. By the time I arrived, he had his backside planted firmly against the front fender of his patrol car and was holding his cowboy hat in his hand. "Good afternoon, Sheriff Joe."

"Will, I have news," he said in a solemn tone. "There is no way to do this but to say it. It is Jenni."

I fell to my knees. I raised my eyes to the sheriff and asked the inevitable question. "Are you sure?"

His reply was just as painful. "Yes, we are sure. DNA testing leaves no doubt. I have some calls to make. Take some time to absorb the news and we will continue talking."

I did not know whether to stand, sit, walk away, or scream. I was lost in a stupor and did not know which way to turn. That made no sense. Why would Jenni be at the end of the road with someone in a car? Was she ever in the car? How could anybody do that to a person as kind as Jenni? I told myself, "Her children have nobody."

After about ten to fifteen minutes, Sheriff Joe exited his patrol car and asked whether I was ready to talk. All I remember telling him is, "I am absolutely lost and do not know what to think or do, but if you have more to tell me, go ahead."

"Understand, now that we have confirmed it is Jenni, CPS has a mountain of paperwork to file on behalf of the children. But you will be allowed a supervised visit," he explained. "We agree with you that the children need to see a familiar, friendly face. All you need to do is go to the CPS offices and they will walk you through all the necessary details." He continued. "Will, if you can think of any other details from that night, call me or come by my office."

That day, as the sheriff drove away from the barn and turned onto the road to leave, I realized that maybe the discomfort I felt whenever I saw his patrol car coming up the road was not anxiety from his impending visit but rather that every time he drove away, loneliness crept into my day. I had been alone for many years of my life and was quite comfortable with solitude, but following the news he just shared, his departure left me with an empty and lonely feeling I had not known since my parents died.

It appeared that Lobo was my only companion that day. He was always by my side when I worked around the house or barn. When I worked in the field, he lay in the shade and watched me work. On this occasion, it was almost like he could sense my despair. As I began the walk back to the house, he fell in line and stayed close on my heels every step. We sat on the porch in silence for a while. He occasionally glanced at me as if he did not understand why we were just sitting. Eventually, I looked at him and said, "It was our Jenni, old boy." He sat up and stared at me with his head cocked a bit to one side. As we sat, I thought of James and Little Jenni and the pain they must have been feeling. When they were told about Jenni, they had no family there to comfort them, only each other.

We sat in silence for a couple of hours, when I decided it was time to face the remainder of the day. I saddled my buckskin mare and rode along the creek to a couple of fenced pastures to check and count cows. As always, Lobo trotted along behind, occasionally changing course to run to the creek for a quick drink. We managed to occupy ourselves until it was time for supper. We returned to the barn, where I removed the buckskin's saddle and brushed her before releasing her to roam the pasture.

CHAPTER SEVEN

Lobo resigned himself to the shade of the porch as I finished mowing the yard. I could see that he had visited the creek for a drink and was wet up to his shoulders. With the days getting shorter, it was not as hot each day and the grass was growing much slower. I hoped that meant it would be the last time I had to mow that year. The activities over the past several weeks since the sheriff's visit had spared no time to do my yard work, which was now a couple of weeks overdue. Mowing had always relaxed me, and it was nice to get back to the routine.

I hoped to finish by lunchtime, watch the noon news, and get myself ready for a trip to the courthouse and my attorney's office. I returned the mowing equipment to the barn and relaxed in a hot bath for a few minutes before turning on the television and preparing my lunch. Although I had filled Lobo's food bowl, he danced around my chair insisting I share my lunch with him. We were almost finished with my lunch when the noon news came on the air and the anchor announced the day's stories. Leading the list was live coverage from the courthouse, where the sheriff was expected to announce a suspect in the Jenni Whittington murder.

With the temperatures a bit cooler, they held the press conference on the steps of the courthouse. A small crowd had gathered to watch as Sheriff Joe, raising a photograph for the television cameras, announced, "We have named a suspect in the Jenni Whittington case, Jake Cummings." Simultaneous to the sheriff's announcement, Channel 8 posted a picture of Jake in the corner of the television screen. The sheriff continued his statement. "We have sufficient evidence to move Jake Cummings from a person of interest to our prime suspect. Also, we have reason to believe he may still be in the area. If you see Jake Cummings, notify my office or your local police. Thank you."

As the reporters on hand shouted their questions, the sheriff turned and began the walk back into the courthouse. One reporter shouted, "Sheriff Joe, is it true there was a witness?"

The sheriff said, "I have no further comment. Thank you."

I thought to myself, "I hope all these people are gone by the time I get there."

It was typically a twenty-minute drive from the farm to the courthouse. That day, I enjoyed the drive and made the trip take even longer. But, to my disappointment, a few reporters were still milling about the courthouse grounds when I arrived. I had no reason to believe my statement to the sheriff and the district attorney had been shared, but I was still hesitant. I considered driving past the courthouse and waiting them out, but it was too important to delay. It was the day I would complete the last of the required paperwork and have my last visit with CPS. Things had been progressing well, meaning it should not be long before I took James and Little Jenni home with me. CPS had allowed me weekly visits with the kids. It had been good for them to see me and share stories of their mom, but even I could see that we were all holding back a lot of pain and sorrow that would eventually boil over. One thing that gave them great comfort was knowing Lobo was safe and happy. I had shared pictures of him during every weekly visit.

I hardly had time to park my old truck and open the door before two reporters were asking questions and hurriedly readying their equipment. One reporter asked whether I had witnessed the murder and whether I had provided a statement to the district attorney. I was a bit surprised and not prepared to respond. I glanced at the reporter as I walked past and turned my attention to the sidewalk in front of me. Maybe the best response was no response. At least I hoped that would prove to be true.

My last official visit with CPS was brief, with only a couple of final forms to complete and sign. I left the office and walked the long hallway to the sheriff's office, entered, and asked Beverly whether Sheriff Joe was still in his office.

Beverly said, "Let me ask if he can see you now." She quickly entered and then exited his office and confirmed he was available for a visit. "Go on in." Standing outside his door, I had heard the entire conversation. I smiled as I thought, "They might as well have just yelled back and forth like they did the last time I was here."

I had not even had a chance to sit when the sheriff said, "Will, if you saw the statement, you know we are looking for Jake. We are prepared to charge him for Jenni's murder, and there are some things I need to let you know. Jenni was at the Longhorn Ranch convenience store that evening. With both of her vehicles being at her farm, we do not know how she got there. We assume she walked. But she was there at the same time as Jake. She first appears on camera as she walked around the corner of the store from the north side of the building, where there is no camera. We have Jake on video filling a small gas can and placing it in the trunk of his car. We have a video of him entering the store, paying for his gas, and speaking with Jenni. Is there any chance Jake knew Jenni?"

I thought for a moment before responding. "I would say there is a good chance he knew Jenni. You know everybody was welcome at our keg parties back in the day. There is a very good chance Jake saw Jenni and me together many times back then."

The sheriff continued. "The reason I ask is, we also have video of Jenni retracing her steps and disappearing from camera view as she walked around the corner of the store. Shortly after that, Jake drove along the west side of the store and disappeared from camera view as he entered the small parking lot on the north side of the store. We think Jenni may have gotten into the car with Jake, but we do not have video confirmation of that."

He continued. "Next, we think Jake may still be in the area. The only reason we can think of that he would be buying gas in such a small can was for a lawn mower. By our reasoning, he is staying with someone near the store. So we are focusing our search for him in the Longhorn Ranch, Route 66 area."

I explained, "I had a reporter ask whether I witnessed the murder or had given a statement to the district attorney. I am not surprised by that, but I need you to understand, if Jake sees or hears that, I can expect a visit from him. He will not let that go without consequence. Sheriff, if Jake shows up at my house, it will not go well for one of us."

His reply surprised me. "Will, you do what you need to do, especially if you have those kids with you." I quickly looked up and began to speak, but he cut me off. "Yes, I know that things are moving along with CPS. Will, I think it is a good thing you are doing with Jenni's kids. You are effectively cleared of any involvement in Jenni's homicide. If you ever need my help with Jenni's children or legal matters, please do not hesitate to ask. I will stand by your side."

"Thank you, Sheriff Joe, I appreciate that." I opened the door and left.

I made my way across the street to my attorney's office for a two o'clock appointment. I had met Bruce the summer my parents died in a car wreck. He handled the immense amount of paperwork required to settle my parents' estate and transfer title of the farm to my name. I had not seen him in a few years, so we took a few minutes to catch up. Eventually, we moved on to the matters at hand. I half commented and half asked, "The court will have to appoint an executor for Jenni's estate, and since I am working with CPS to get custody of the children, it would probably be best if I was the executor." I also explained that, according to the letter Jenni had left behind, I am James's father. "Regardless of who serves as executor, when CPS gives me custody of James and Little Jenni, I will have you file adoption papers for me."

I continued. "Of course what I think is only my opinion, but I think keeping Jenni's farm in a trust for James and Little Jenni would be best. My intention would be to move the children to my farm, with extended visits to Jenni's place a couple of times each year. My plan would be to move her few cattle to my farm and run them with my herd. I will raise row crops at her place, hopefully earning enough to keep the property for the kids when they are grown and can do with it as they may."

Bruce said, "Will, you have never farmed row crops in your life."

"I know, but I am known for working like a mule to do the things I say I will do. I will do whatever it takes, work whatever hours are required, to keep that place for Jenni's kids."

Bruce chuckled. "Yes, you are known to be a hard worker and hardheaded like a mule."

"The last matter I need help with is the estate. If Jenni did not have a last will and testament, I need you to handle probate for the kids. I will find a way to pay you even if I must sell some cows to get the money."

Bruce rose from his chair and extended his hand. I shook his hand as he said, "Will, I will investigate the executor issue first. I will investigate the trust as well. Let's deal with the remaining issues as they arise. You let me know how things are progressing with CPS and custody of the children."

Walking to my truck, I thought about Bruce. It seems you never know who you might meet living in any small town across the country. A few years ago, Bruce had asked me to build a new bookcase and cabinet for his law office. As I'd cleared the old shelves and a couple of old file cabinets to make room for the new, I saw numerous law journal articles written by him. Later, I told Bruce, "I was not snooping and being nosey, but I noticed several articles and publications with your name on them." He somewhat reluctantly replied, "Yes, I have had some articles published. Before moving here in the early nineteen eighties, I was a law professor at the University of Tulsa law school. I was published many times and wrote and edited numerous textbooks. I have continued to write since coming here. I have just enough ego that I think everybody should know my opinion on things." He'd laughed at that last part.

We parted with a handshake and a commitment to speak again soon.

Chapter Eight

As I drove my old tractor to the field to clear some underbrush along the creek, my mind began to wander as I visually relived memories of prom night so many years ago. The thoughts of when my friendship with Jake became soured ran through my mind.

It was prom night 1988, and Jenni and I were one of the popular couples in our local high school. I was dressed in a rented tuxedo, as was the custom for prom night, and Jenni was wearing a stunning blue dress purchased for the occasion. We had laughed a few weeks earlier as I jokingly told her to pick a dress that was a bit more revealing, but her mom was not laughing. It did not matter to me what she chose to wear; she was the prettiest girl in school, or anywhere around. The prom committee rented a ballroom at a local resort for the event. The room was decorated in blue and red with several signs, banners, and streamers scattered about. As you would expect, "Senior 1988" was the theme. Jenni was on the prom decorating committee, and I tried to brag about the decorations every chance I got. She was proud of the committee's efforts and accomplishments. I took as many pictures of the decorations as I did of our classmates.

We were in love and had great hopes for a future together, but there was tension in the air. I would soon graduate and start college, and Jenni would still be in high school. She had her concerns about enduring that transition and us staying together. We were both country kids, and neither of us had any inclination toward moving away to go to college or seeking advanced college degrees. I knew what the future held for me. I would spend my life working a cattle farm and work as a carpenter when opportunities presented themselves. But I knew I needed to take several college courses to better prepare for operating a farm as a business. Times were changing, requiring an understanding of how to manage money and inventory like any other business. Jenni's plan was to graduate high school and attend the local community college as well. She hoped to pursue a nursing certificate so she could work at one of the nearby hospitals. Jenni knew I would be living at home and commuting to the local community college, not trying to keep our relationship alive over a long distance, but she was concerned. I reassured her on many occasions that I would still be at her house every day and we would still spend our free time together. Yet she remained nervous that our relationship would not be able to survive with me being in college. But we agreed on one thing: we would enjoy this night.

We spent the evening moving around the room, speaking with the other couples at the prom. Graduation was looming on the horizon, and this would be the last time we had with many of our classmates. We may have even danced a slow song or two as the disco ball cast various colored reflections around the room. It did not seem that the evening had lasted long, but the house lights came on and our prom chaperones announced it was time to close the evening.

As planned, we stopped at Jenni's house to change clothes and go to the annual prom party. I reassured Jenni's mom and dad that we would not get into any trouble and that I would take care of their daughter. Her mom called me to the kitchen to talk. She told me, "Will, you and Jenni are special, and what you share is special. You know I think of you like family, and like family, I know you will go to any length to protect Jenni."

I reassured her that Jenni was the love of my life and the most special person I knew. "There is nothing I will not do to protect her," I said.

They knew we were going to a keg party but trusted that we would not overindulge. Other than the time we spent at Cain's Bayou, we were always very straightforward with her parents about what we were doing or not doing. I always believed in being honest with them. I wanted them to know exactly where I was taking their only child and never let there be any surprises.

We both enjoyed the camaraderie of the keg parties, but neither of us was the party type. We both thought of the parties as a chance to be around our classmates, share old memories, and laugh with our friends. We occasionally gave a ride to someone who was in no condition to drive. And if they needed, I would pick them up the next day to return them to collect their vehicle. I did not know whether it was the excitement of it being prom night or some other celestial event, but some of our classmates were a little rowdier than usual. There had been some arguing and yelling, but that was normal. As the night wound down, a fight broke out between an underclassman and Jake Cummings. Jake was a hell-raiser and loved to stir up trouble wherever he went. But this was not a fair fight. I jumped into the fray to stop Jake. He took a swing at me but missed wildly. I had managed to stop the fight, but that just caused Jake to turn his attention to me. "Come on, Will. I am not afraid of you," he yelled.

I said, "You are drunk and do not need to be fighting someone that much smaller than you. The world hates a bully, and you are being a bully." Again, he took a wild swing at me and missed. I shoved him to the ground and barked at him, "Not tonight, Jake."

It was then that I heard Jenni screaming, "Stop, Will. It is not worth it to fight him."

As I turned to walk away, Jake shouted, "We are not through here."

I said, "We are through for tonight."

As he picked himself up off the ground and slapped the dust from his clothes, Jake said, "We will finish this another day, another time."

Without turning to look at him, I said, "Another day will be fine with me."

Jenni grabbed my arm and said, "It is time for us to leave. Let's go to Cain's Bayou."

I had not noticed until then, but it was a full moon that night. It occurred to me that it may have been the reason for so many issues at the keg party. It did not matter what issues were happening around us because, when we went to Cain's Bayou, we left all conflict behind. When we'd first found this secluded part of the lake, we had agreed this was "our spot" and we would never fight or argue when we were there.

We climbed onto the hood of my truck and lay with our backs against the windshield. Jenni laid her head on my shoulder, and we relaxed and talked. Jenni said, "I wish we could stay like this forever. I know we cannot, and life will never be this simple again, but at this moment, Will, I love you. I always will."

Talking was what we did at Cain's Bayou. We may have both wanted to be intimate, but we both realized, even at that young age, there was more to being in love than a physical relationship. We both realized that sex could bring about many complications that change lives in unwanted ways. Our ambitions may have been simple, but we wanted to create a better life for ourselves. So we just talked and stared at the reflection of the full moon across the surface of the water. I jumped down for a moment and grabbed an old blanket I kept behind the seat of my truck. It may have been springtime, but being by the water with a breeze blowing, the night air had developed a chill. I returned to the hood of the truck and placed the blanket over Jenni. She felt so comfortable in my arms. It just felt natural, like it was meant to be. We spent a couple of hours reflecting on when we first met and how far we had come since then.

CHAPTER NINE

As my long day came to an end and the sun began to fade behind the hill to the west, I knew I had a few things left to do. It had only been a couple of days since the sheriff's announcement that Jake was the number-one suspect in Jenni's murder, and since the reporter had asked whether there was a witness, I expected a visit from Jake. There was an old Ford F-9 tractor I had been intending to repair for several years parked on the back side of the barn. My intentions may have been to repair it and use it for lighter-duty work on the farm, but I had only accomplished creating a spot for weeds to grow. I jumped on another tractor, hooked a chain to the old F-9 tractor, pulled it to the front yard, and turned it broadside to the house. My goal was to park it where the motion-sensor floodlight attached to the soffit on the southeast corner of the house would shine directly on it. I retrieved a handful of nine-millimeter shells from my pocket, placed them in the toolbox under the seat of the old tractor, and secured the latch.

I took a water bowl and some hard food to the barn for Lobo. He had become accustomed to spending his nights in the house, but that night he would be visiting the "Rogers Barn Resort." I fashioned a long leash for him, but not quite long enough for him to get outside the doorway of the barn. I did not want him outside the barn and in danger of being shot. As I flipped the switch to turn on the lights outside the barn, he whimpered and slowly lay down as he watched me walk away. Back inside the house, I turned on both outside lights on the back side of the house and locked the doors. I donned my nine-millimeter and holster, grabbed and loaded my Henry 30-30 lever-action rifle, and made myself comfortable in my easy chair.

It was surprisingly quiet as I sat and waited for Lobo to bark. If Jake came for a visit, he would most likely approach the house from the north. My hope was that if he did approach from the north, the lights on the barn and Lobo's barking would force him to take a different route to the house. With the backyard lights and my old pole light lighting the backyard, he would have to swing wide toward the road and approach the house from the front—the only accessible unlit area for him to approach. I was confident he would not approach from the south since he would be forced to wade the creek. If he indeed approached from the front and got close to the house, the floodlight would force him to take cover behind the old Ford tractor. All I had to do was wait for Lobo to start barking and wait for the floodlight to come on. I knew I could then go out the south door, which would now be the only unlit area around the house, take cover at the corner of the house or well house, and see what happened. Jake would be blinded by the floodlight and would only be able to see my muzzle flash. If anything other than that happened and I needed cover, I could hide behind the old tractor, where I had stashed extra ammunition.

At 1:37 a.m., I looked at the clock and asked myself, "Are you being just a bit paranoid?" It was not long after that I caught myself as my head drooped and I was dozing off. That is when Lobo broke the silence of the night. His bark was louder and more intense than I had heard before. So I waited. I did not watch the clock, but I would guess it was about four minutes or so later when the floodlight came on. I was somewhat blurry-eyed but gazed out the window toward the old tractor. I was not sure whether my eyes were simply adjusting to the light, but I thought I saw movement under the tractor. Still carrying my Henry rifle, and with my nine-millimeter on my hip, I raced out the south door and slipped into the darkness of the night. As I crept to the corner of the house to investigate, I realized I did not have the cover I had anticipated. So I moved to the well house. Even at that angle, the light would provide some cover for me. I lay on my stomach with the barrel of my Henry rifle angled around the corner of the well house and waited for any sign of movement.

It was not long before Jake's words rang out. "Come out, Will. Let's get this over with. I did not do anything to

Jenni, but this is the road you and Sheriff Joe have decided to take. We have some old business to take care of anyway."

I continued to wait quietly. I knew that every time he looked toward the house, it would take several seconds for his eyes to adjust to the darkness around us.

"I know you can hear me. Come out," he shouted.

I remained quiet. The light shone brightly on the old tractor, but beyond that was a veil of endless darkness my eyes could not penetrate. Where I could normally see the silhouette of the trees against the night sky was just darkness. The floodlight suddenly turned off, my advantage of the darkness gone. I was instantly consumed with fear. I had one hope: if he tried to leave the protection of the tractor, the light would come back on. I waited quietly but shaking. After what seemed to be about five minutes, the light turned on and I caught a glimpse of Jake as he scurried back to the cover of the tractor. I also spotted light reflecting from what appeared to be the barrel of a nickel-plated handgun. I felt confident he was still unaware that I was lying only fifteen to twenty yards away. I lined up my sights with the lower part of the right rear tire of the tractor and waited. I had decided that if I saw anything move, I would pull the trigger. Neither of us made a noise. Then I saw a leg, hip, shoulder, or something move just above where I had kept my rifle's sights. I squeezed the trigger. The rifle fire echoed through the valley, but I did not hear any reaction from Jake. I knew that hammering the lever-action rifle would surely give away my position. So I slowly slid my

Henry rifle to the ground by my side and unholstered my nine-millimeter. Again, I waited in silence. I was confident the floodlight had helped hide my location, but I could not count on that with too many shots. I slid a bit farther around the corner of the well house and maintained a ready-to-fire position with my nine-millimeter. At the next sign of movement, I would fire again.

Jake and I had been in this position before, facing each other with guns drawn, and I had been hesitant to pull the trigger then. "This time, he knows I am serious, not afraid, and willing to fire," I thought to myself. I aimed my nine-millimeter at the same area I had focused my rifle on minutes earlier and waited for movement. Again, I saw something slide out from behind the tractor tire. I gently squeezed the trigger. Even as the sharp report of the shot echoed through the valley, I heard an odd deep moan. "My shot was true," I told myself.

I waited quietly. I could not hear any sound coming from the old tractor, just Lobo barking frantically from the barn. I waited for what seemed like an hour. The floodlight had gone off and had not come back on for a while. I decided to check to see if Jake was wounded or dead. Knowing that as I approached the tractor, the floodlight would come on and I would be an easy, lit-up target, I slowly crawled around the corner of the well house and toward the tractor. I was probably ten feet from it when the floodlight lit up that small part of the yard and the tractor again. I stopped and stared at the tractor. I could easily see the top, the bottom, and under the tractor. I did not see anything. I rose to my feet, assumed a firing position with my nine-millimeter, and approached the tractor. Nothing. No Jake. Just the long shadow of the tractor. He had disappeared into the night.

"How did he slip away?" I asked myself. Then I saw car lights come on and taillights glowing red about one-half mile down the valley. I quickly realized Jake had parked his vehicle in a notch in the timber. Years ago, during installation of electrical lines, the power company had cleared some timber to gain access to the ridge where the power lines would run. It was an obvious location to hide a vehicle.

It only took me a minute to decide this must be finished tonight. I would not let this continue, especially knowing Jenni's kids would live there soon. I raced into the house to retrieve the keys to my old truck. I flipped the light switch as I entered the house, grabbed my keys, and turned to race out the door when I noticed something red on my boot. I bent down to look and was certain it was blood. "I did hit him," I thought. I grabbed my flashlight as I ran out the door to the old tractor and searched the ground. Sure enough, there was a significant amount of blood on the grass.

If there had ever been a time I needed my old farm truck to be dependable, this was it. All it did was crank. I yelled out loud, "Of all the times for you not to start. I might as well be trying to drive that old dead tractor." Finally, just as I thought my battery was about to die, the old truck fired and I was ready to go. As I slammed my old truck into reverse and began to back out of the driveway, I remembered my

Henry rifle—I might need a long gun. I retrieved the rifle, got back into the truck, and started down the road. I had the old truck flying down those country roads in pursuit. "This will end tonight," I repeated again and again in my mind. I had lost so much time before getting on the road I worried I would not be able to catch Jake, but I would try. About a mile from the highway, I crested the hill and saw nothing but red and blue lights ahead.

With the red and blue lights swirling and flashing, it was hard to recognize Jake's car, but I was sure it was in the middle of the patrol cars. I rolled my old truck to the side of the road and parked. I expected deputies to push me away from the area, but none confronted me. I maintained a distance and watched. Everyone moved calmly and without any apparent urgency. After a couple of minutes, I saw Sheriff Joe walking toward me.

As he approached, Sheriff Joe said, "Will, it is over. You will not have any future issues with Jake Cummings."

"That is a great relief. I did not want to always be on the lookout for him, especially if Jenni's kids are at my place."

Sheriff Joe noticed the holster and weapon on my hip. "Is that the nine-millimeter I saw that night at your house?"

"Yes, sir."

"Will, there is nothing you need to be here for. You should go home."

A deputy waving his flashlight around like a Fourth of July sparkler approached. "Sheriff Joe, from what we can see with him still in the car, he suffered three gunshot wounds."

As I turned my focus from the deputy to Sheriff Joe and began to tell him that Jake had been at my house, the deputy's flashlight shone across my boot. The sheriff and I looked up at the same time and our eyes locked. "Will, one of your neighbors reported gunfire. My deputies immediately knew what was occurring and were en route to your place when they saw Jake's car stopped in the road. Listen to me now. My deputies, both carrying nine-millimeter service weapons, approached Jake's vehicle and could clearly see a weapon. Jake was unwilling to exit his vehicle and surrender his weapon. Ultimately, they felt their lives were in danger and fired on the vehicle and suspect. They apparently struck him three times. One of those shots was fatal. That is what my statement to the press will be. And I assume they will be here sooner rather than later. Go home." As he walked away, he turned and said, "Get rid of those boots."

CHAPTER TEN

The bright-orange note on the refrigerator read, "October 27 CPS 8:00." I had poured a cup of coffee and pulled the note from the refrigerator door as I walked past. The note had occupied this space on the door for some weeks at this point, and I was ready to take it down. I was not sure I needed another cup of coffee that morning, but I am not a person who drifts too far from my routine.

I tried sitting in my easy chair to drink my coffee. I tried sitting at the table to drink my coffee. It became obvious to me that it did not matter where I was sitting; I was nervous and was going to fidget. I knew I had prepared the kids' rooms for them. They had beds and furniture. I thought I had everything in order but could not calm my nerves. The events transpiring that day would change lives, and I was ready to get it underway.

Even though I was nervous, my drive was pleasant and comfortable. Autumn may be my favorite time of the year. The tree leaves had begun changing color, creating palettes of pastel landscapes, and many of the pastures in the area were freshly mowed from the last hay cutting of the year. The sun seemed clearer and brighter, the air clear and crisp. That day, the early-morning sunlight lit up the dew on the grass, making acres of tiny, diamond-like reflections. As I enjoyed the sights of the morning, I remembered my grandfather, a full-blood Cherokee, telling me to enjoy and embrace the changing seasons. He explained, "The changes you will endure in this life are like the changes in seasons. Like the seasons, life will always change. You cannot prevent the changes in life, like you cannot stop the constant change of the seasons. That will never end. Whether you embrace those changes or resist them will determine your happiness in life." Like the onset of autumn, I embraced the coming change. It was going to be a beautiful day.

I had visited the courthouse so many times over the past couple of months I had become familiar with the location of just about all county offices. I could have made the walk to CPS with my eyes closed. I knew that when I walked through their door, my life would not be the same. I opened the door and stepped inside. The place was different that day. The staff had decorated the office with various decorations and had banners with the kids' names hanging below another banner that read, "Congratulations!" The staff was all smiles for this occasion. These were not the normal circumstances they worked through when dealing with displaced children, and it was obvious they were pleased with the outcome of this case. It was as if they had cleared their calendar for the morning and had time to devote to us alone. I was not told, "Have a seat. We'll be with you in a minute." I was greeted with handshakes and hugs.

It was a brief meeting. I do not know whether it was standard protocol, but I received some simple instructions regarding procedure and reporting of any issues. The staff repeated that if any issues arose, call them. If I needed any services related to the children, call them. There were a surprising number of reasons to call them.

They brought James and Little Jenni into the offices momentarily. Shelley Corntassel, the CPS director, asked them if they were ready to go home with me. Both replied with an enthusiastic, "Yes, ma'am." Shelley opened the swinging gate separating their offices from the waiting area, and they walked into the room with me. I knelt down and hugged and held them for a minute as James and Little Jenni began to cry. The staff cried. As I felt a tear stream down my cheek, I rose from my kneeling position. I lifted James in my left arm and Little Jenni in my right as they both placed their arms around my neck. I thanked the staff for all they had done for us, looked at the children, and said, "Just hang on to me. We will be all right. Let's go home."

When we arrived at the farm, I knew the first order of business was Lobo. This was a new home for the kids, and Lobo would provide some comfort of familiarity. I opened the door to let Lobo outside. He bolted past me and into the welcoming arms of James and Little Jenni. Lobo could not contain himself. He jumped from James to Little Jenni and back again in a much-needed reunion. We sat on the porch with Lobo for a while before going into the house.

I walked the kids through the house and showed them their rooms. I explained we could paint their rooms any color and decorate however they wanted. I told them, "This is your home. If you need or want something, you must tell me. This is something new for you. It is also something new for me. We will figure this out and get through it together. How about if we just walk around the farm today and let Lobo celebrate some time with you? Later today or tomorrow, if you would like, we will go to your house and get some clothes, toys, whatever you want or need. This evening, some friends, Josh and Amy, will visit for a cookout. I want you to meet them because you will spend a lot of time with them in the future." They nodded their approval of the plan.

We walked through the barn and covered most of the farm. We walked along the creek, skipped rocks across a pond, and talked. I told them stories of when their mom and I were young and about the great times we had shared. I took them to places on the farm that Jenni and I had enjoyed together. I showed them the swimming hole where we had spent so many hours swimming, splashing, and laughing. It was apparent this was something I would be doing often. Of course, I only shared the fun and romantic stories. But I realized, as they get older, someday I would have to tell the story about the night on Route 66.

How this day was going to unfold had probably run through my mind a hundred times since I learned they were coming to live with me. Of course, nothing I had envisioned actually occurred. This was better.

CHAPTER ELEVEN

One notable thing from the fall and the beginning of the winter season was frequent visits from Sheriff Joe. I was not surprised when he visited the first time. I assumed CPS had asked him to stop by when he was in my part of the county. After a couple more drop-by visits from him, I was beginning to question the intent. During one of his visits, he asked, "Will, what caused the rift between you and Jake?"

I described the events from prom night years ago, explaining that I had always felt that Jake and I were friends but was not sure that anybody was ever really friends with Jake. I told him, "Jake had an evil side. Being around Jake was like standing at the edge of a cliff. If you were not careful, you could fall. But with Jake, if you fell, you would fall into an abyss, an abyss of violence. Jake lived in a world of violence, and I tried to stay out of Jake's world." I asked the sheriff, "Have you ever heard the farmers' old saying, 'Life is easier if you learn to plow around the stumps'? Well,

Jake was a stump to be plowed around. He was someone to avoid if possible."

Sheriff Joe then asked about the incident from years previous, when Jake and I had an encounter in town. I explained, "Jake and a friend of mine were having what seemed like a minor disagreement in the parking lot of the local grocery store, but knowing Jake, I assumed it was likely to get out of hand. So I got between them and tried to break the tension. The next thing I knew, Jake had a gun pointed at me and, needless to say, was threatening to shoot me. To Jake's surprise, I pulled a small-caliber handgun from my beltline. We stood facing each other, maybe thirty feet apart, with pistols aimed at each other. Knowing Jake, I was sure he intended to pull the trigger, and I really did not want to be shot. It is surprising how many thoughts run through your mind at a time like that. My main thought at that time was whether me shooting him was going to be justified in the eyes of the law. I did not know the answer to that question but was determined not to be shot. As I began to gently squeeze the trigger, Jake threw his hands in the air and said, 'My gun is not loaded.' When he released the clip from his automatic, I tucked my pistol back into my beltline. As I was getting into my car to drive away, I told Jake, 'That is a good way to get yourself shot.' I have never understood how it escalated so quickly from a simple intervention to guns being drawn."

After that visit, I began to question whether Sheriff Joe wanted to become friends, was simply verifying the kids and I were getting along, or maybe was visiting to report to CPS. Regardless, I was sure he was stopping by CPS and giving them updates on his way back to his office. That was fine by me. We were probably doing better than could be expected. He never asked probing questions or seemed to be fishing for information, but I just could not silence that little voice that kept telling me there was something more to his visits. I assumed his office had ballistics reports on the bullets from Jake's body and was aware that one bullet did not match the deputies' service weapons. That left me a bit on edge and unwilling to voluntarily share information from the night of Jake's visit.

At the conclusion of one of his visits, he asked me to follow him to his patrol car. To my surprise, he said, "Beverly, my deputies, and the folks from CPS pitched in to get the kids some Christmas gifts." He opened the trunk of his patrol car, which was stuffed full of gift bags and wrapped boxes. He said, "There are dolls, toys, clothes, shoes, and school supplies. All the gifts are wrapped, but they have the kids' names on them so you will know who gets each gift. I told all my staff that if you are like me, someone better wrap the gifts before we deliver them." We quickly shuffled them to my old truck. The smile on his face revealed an entirely different side of him than I had ever seen. I made a mental note that the kids and I would have to do something for them. Maybe we could host a picnic at the farm and they could bring their kids for a hayride and wienie roast.

CHAPTER TWELVE

The kids and I got along well through the fall and into winter. There were lots of good times and some rocky spots, lots of walks around the farm, and stories about Jenni. They had their favorite stories, and I told those many times. They understood, even at their young ages, that their mom was special to me. It must have been obvious from the stories I told and things I said that Jenni held a special place in my heart—that and I said it many, many times.

The holidays were rough times, as I assumed they would be. I had decided we would spend Thanksgiving at the farm and Christmas at Jenni's house. By the time Thanksgiving rolled around, they had learned that I could make a mean sandwich or scrambled eggs, and could manage my way around a grill, but a full-fledged Thanksgiving meal was going to be a stretch for me. I explained that they would have to pitch in and help. We spent the morning of Thanksgiving Day in the kitchen, slipping, tripping, and stumbling over each other as we prepared our afternoon feast. I had placed a turkey in the oven earlier in the morning, and we prepared the traditional side dishes. Although the turkey turned out well and the dressing was okay, the act of cooking had been chaos, but it was fun with the kids. The kitchen looked like an Oklahoma tornado had hit it by the time we finished. There was flour, water, breadcrumbs, and vegetables scattered across the countertops and the floor. But we managed, enjoyed a big lunch, and cleaned the mess. I told them the best part of the Thanksgiving meal was yet to come. I told them if they had never had leftover turkey sandwiches after Thanksgiving, I was going to introduce them to a culinary treat. In unison, they remarked, "No, not more sandwiches." We all laughed.

I knew Christmas at Jenni's was going to be hard to get through, but I wanted our first one together to be at the location where they had shared every previous Christmas. I let them know they would have to guide me through the holiday and show me how they celebrated Christmas. We went to the house early enough on Christmas Eve to retrieve their tree and decorations from the attic. We decorated the tree like they had with Jenni, or at least as best we could. I thought it looked pretty good for an amateur and two small children.

Maybe it is odd, but I could not force myself to sleep in Jenni's bed. So I told James and Little Jenni we should all make a pallet on the floor and sleep in the living room. But then I realized that might be a problem for Santa. I explained to them that if we were in the living room with the Christmas tree, Santa might not be able to visit and leave presents, so we should sleep in one of their rooms. They agreed and we all slept in Little Jenni's room. It worked out well for me. I could not sleep in Jenni's bed and had no intention of being away from the kids in case there were any bad dreams or issues during the night. We had made several visits to their house since they moved to my farm, and being there was getting easier for them, but I knew Christmas would be different.

I was awakened by screams of delight that Santa had visited during the night and there were presents under the tree. I am not a guy who promotes the concept of Santa Claus, but Jenni did, so I honored what she believed. But that Christmas, there was a Santa Claus. He even left a little something for me under the tree, a picture of Jenni, James, and Little Jenni. It was from a vacation trip they had taken, and all three were dressed like bank robbers from the 1800s.

They opened their presents and told me how much they missed their mom and, as expected, cried a lot. They talked about Christmas presents they had received over the past few years. They groaned with displeasure when I told them I would cook us breakfast with scrambled eggs, sausage, and some fresh biscuits. I carried on like this was a big deal, but I cooked the same breakfast every Sunday before church. It had become a joke with us. After breakfast, we cleared the table and washed and dried the dishes. I told them to grab some blankets and we could pile up on the couch and watch television. As they rushed to Little Jenni's room to get blankets and pillows, I turned on the television. But as soon as they were on the couch, wrapped up and warm, I turned the television off and asked them to share their favorite Christmas memories with me.

They had funny stories and a couple of sad stories. Jenni had endured a couple of lonely years that really brought her down. Only her strength and her two kids got her through those years. They told of one Christmas that Jenni had talked about me and the times we had shared. She showed them her favorite necklace. She told them it had been a Christmas gift from me when we were teenagers. They said it was just after that Christmas when I came to their house for the first time and they met me. I asked James if he could find that necklace and bring it to me. A couple of minutes later, James returned from Jenni's room and handed it to me. I told him how proud Jenni would have been that he was so helpful.

I asked Little Jenni to sit in front of me, and I placed the necklace around her neck and told her, "I know that Jenni would want you to have this. This was her gift at Christmas many years ago, and this Christmas it is yours. You are so much like she was when we were younger." I told them about the day I gave Jenni the necklace, how pretty she looked, and how excited she was to get the necklace. At this point, I had learned two things that were particularly meaningful to the kids: to tell Little Jenni how much she was like her mom, and to tell James how proud Jenni would be of him and how he helped take care of his little sister. I guess I believed it would create visual images of Jenni and her beautiful smile in their minds.

A couple of days after Christmas, we received a good snowfall, about eight inches. James and Little Jenni grew up on the prairie and had never been snow sledding. So I dug an old sled out of the barn, dressed them as warmly as I could, and up the hill we went. I told them my children and I always went sledding when it snowed. They were shocked to learn that I had children of my own and had many questions. So, as we walked, I told them I had been married and had two children. I met my kids' mom, Julie, when I was in college and we had two kids, a boy and a girl just like them. Now, my daughter was nineteen and my son was eighteen. I explained that Julie and I had been divorced for several years and my kids visited and spent their summers at the farm for a while but had stopped the visits when they got older. I told them maybe, while they were out of school for the summer, my kids would visit. "I know they really want to meet you."

I had one additional surprise for them. Josh and Amy had brought a sled and were going to spend the day with us. They were already at the top of the hill and were waiting for us. Josh, Amy, and I took turns going down the hill with James or Little Jenni on our backs. We all hoped Amy would cook us dinner that evening and the kids could have a break from leftover turkey sandwiches. I told them with a laugh, "Maybe Amy will teach you to cook and we can quit eating sandwiches all the time." We all laughed as I told them, "I am serious." We laughed some more. Although I had expanded my skills to include a variety of meals, we had hopes for something better from Amy. It felt good to see them laugh. It was getting easier for them to relax and be themselves around me. I guess things were beginning to feel more natural for me as well.

Amy and I never spoke about it openly, but I was sure she understood how important she was to Little Jenni and me. Amy knew I was not a guy who talked much or shared a lot, and Little Jenni would need a woman in her life to explain things to her that I was not equipped to handle. Having a strong woman around would be good for James as well. Typically, during their visits, Josh and I would talk about the farm or sports while Amy visited and played with the kids. Following their visits, it was easy to see the impact it had on the kids. James and Little Jenni always, without exception, were happier from their time with Amy. One episode demonstrated that clearly.

Although James and Little Jenni missed their mom and had an occasional period of sorrow, we had managed to get through them. But recently, Little Jenni had an episode I could not help her work through. She was inconsolable. No matter what I tried to do for her, I could not ease her pain. I simply did not have the words she needed to hear. I could not provide the comfort she needed to feel. She was not the happy, well-behaved child I was accustomed to. As soon as I called to ask for help, Amy came to the farm for a visit. She spent the better part of the day with Little Jenni. They sat in Little Jenni's room and talked. They sat on the creek bank and talked. They walked around the yard and talked. Little Jenni clung to Amy, and they cried. They cried a lot. But at the end of the day, Little Jenni was calm. I could tell she was still in pain, but she walked over to James and hugged him, and they ran to the barn to play.

For whatever reason, Amy never shared with me what the episode was about. That information stayed between the two of them. I never doubted that Amy would have shared the details with me if she felt I needed to know.

CHAPTER THIRTEEN

We had promised to host a wienie roast and hayride for all the folks from the sheriff's office and CPS. That day, we were going to deliver on our promise. James and Little Jenni enjoyed the afternoon spent preparing the barn and picnic area by the creek for the evening fun. Of course, the kids loved every opportunity they got to ride on the tractor, and we spent some time getting it ready. We connected the trailer, drove into the barn, and loaded loose hay into the bed of the trailer. We spent a couple of hours walking through the timber, gathering wood, and kindling for a bonfire. We even hauled some regular cut firewood to the spot where our bonfire would be. We gathered some long wienie-roasting rods and cleaned them to a brilliant shine. We hauled all our lawn chairs to the site and placed them in a circle around our firepit. The drinks were on ice, and all the necessary fixins were on the picnic table. We were ready for our guests.

Our firepit is located by the creek, about fifty feet west of the barn, nestled into an area where the creek makes a ninety-degree bend before running along the ridge to the north. The flow of the water slows through the bend and then runs faster as it begins a straight run. The water creates a gentle, soothing, rippling sound as it rushes over the rocky creek bottom. James, Little Jenni, and I had spent several evenings staring into a campfire while listening to the water rush by in the background. I would tell stories from my childhood and stories about Jenni as we watched the fires release their hot embers, drifting upward into the darkness.

Folks no longer do hayrides like they did ages ago, so this was going to be a unique event for the children and grandchildren of those who helped us so much over the past several months. Of course, Josh and Amy would be there too. We picked a weekend during early spring, when the evening air would be cool and being around a fire would take some of the chill away. We asked everybody to arrive around four o'clock. That would give us time to get a fire going, roast some hot dogs, and make s'mores before the darkness of night settled in. We even set up a small grating to cook some hamburgers on a smaller fire to the side.

Shelley Corntassel and her two children were the first to arrive. Her girls were a few years older than James but were a welcome sight for James and Little Jenni. Other than Sheriff Joe, we had not had many visitors since they arrived at the farm, especially not young children. James and Little

Jenni immediately took the girls in tow and were running everywhere. Shelley yelled her warnings for the girls to stay out of the creek. "Do not get wet," she cried out.

Shelley seemed to have something on her mind but was not saying much beyond small talk. So I asked, "Shelley, I assume Sheriff Joe has been providing updates on the kids for you? I assure you, James and Little Jenni are adjusting well. Knowing that I do not have to watch for Jake Cummings every minute of the day and night makes things a bit easier for me. I can keep my focus on the kids and begin to give them some freedom to explore the farm."

She replied, "Yes, the sheriff tells me when he has been for a visit. He has been so impressed with how James and Little Jenni have settled into life with you. Will, I spent a lot of time with them while they were with CPS. They told me many stories about Jenni. They told me that over the past couple of years, she spoke about you many times. I think that gave them a sense of trust in you. I believe the three of you are going to be just fine." She added, "But more than that, I think Jenni was hoping you two would be together again, and the children understood that."

I had not discussed Jenni's letter with anyone other than Sheriff Joe but explained it to Shelley. "Something that has haunted me for months now was a line in a letter Jenni wrote to me. The last line of her letter referred to a night we spent together shortly before she married Scott Barro. She said that we created a child, the greatest gift we could share. I have not stopped asking myself whether the phrase 'the greatest gift we could share' meant she thought we might be together again. Of course, those thoughts only make the pain of her absence more painful."

Over the next thirty minutes or so, Sheriff Joe, the deputies, Beverly, and some of Shelley's CPS staff arrived with their families. The parents found a seat around the fire, some with children clinging to their side. The other children had been running in every direction but were beginning to return to the bonfire. Some had wet shoes and pant legs. Sometimes children find it hard to resist the temptation of playing along the creek, and accidents are going to happen. The children began roasting wienies as I cooked hamburgers for the adults. Although a couple of wienies fell from the rods and were sacrificed to the fire or a bit overcooked, the kids enjoyed roasting them.

As everybody was finishing their campfire dinner, several of the children prepared and enjoyed s'mores. I started my Ford tractor and parked it between the barn and the fire. We loaded the children, a couple of parents, and Amy into the trailer and drove them across the creek and into a small pasture, across the creek again, and through the pasture to the north. At first, they were very quiet, but as we moved farther into the field, they began to laugh and scream whenever we hit a bump and they bounced from their makeshift seats. I could hear Amy as she laughed and joked with the children. Darkness was settling in as I eased the tractor to a spot beside the creek a short distance from the bonfire.

The fire was now providing a red glow, creating a pocket of light within the darkness of night.

The evening air was becoming cool as we nestled around the fire. We discussed the weather, high school sports, local politics, and the children. The conversation was free-flowing, which was good to see. I had learned over the years that some folks are just not comfortable with silence, and I had some concerns the night might get stale and awkward for some. I had noticed something about Sheriff Joe when he arrived and decided this was a good time to ask him about it. "Sheriff Joe, I realized something this evening that had never occurred to me. I have known you for several years now, and I do not believe I have ever seen you out of uniform or without your badge."

He thought for a moment and then replied. "Will, there is never a time that I am not the sheriff. I may not be on duty, but I am always the sheriff. I do not get to turn that off. Even on days that I am off duty, if I see an issue or crime, I will respond. And if I must respond in an official capacity, I want everybody to realize who I am and that I am not a civilian intervening. The only times you would see me without my badge displayed is if I am outside the county. I do not get to spend much vacation time inside the county."

Shelley Corntassel joined the discussion. "That is interesting. I had never thought about that. So you almost never get to be off duty."

"No," Sheriff Joe replied. "Understand, I love what I do. This job allows me to help people in so many different ways. I cannot imagine giving up this job. But yes, I am on duty twenty-four hours per day, every day. I have seen some horrific things, but I have also seen things that would melt your heart. I have seen the worst of people, but I have seen the best of people. I have been told many times that I should write a book about my experiences."

"Do you think you would ever write a book?" Shelley asked.

Without hesitation, Sheriff Joe replied. "No, I could not do that. I have thought about it on occasion, but it is something I just could not do. Yes, there are many stories I could write that people might find interesting, but the details of those stories could embarrass and hurt people. They could hurt friends of mine and maybe even friends of yours. There are details that will go to the grave with me."

Abe, a man from CPS, asked, "Even if you could make money from a book, you would not do it?"

Sheriff Joe repeated, "There are things that will go to the grave with me. There is no amount of money worth changing that."

We called all the children to join us by the fire for stories. Sheriff Joe and I told ghost stories, stories that passed from generation to generation. Storytelling was a tradition in my family. Anytime we gathered at night, we listened to my grandfather tell ghost stories. I may not possess his storytelling ability, but I told the stories I had heard so many

times during my childhood. Sheriff Joe had some great stories I had never heard before. That was a great way to wind
down the evening. I noticed that James and Little Jenni had
found their way to my side. I thought they were looking for
a little comfort from the chill of the evening, or maybe a
chill from the stories.

With them by my side, I stood. "If you are here, it is
because, over the past several months, you have played an
important role in the lives of James and Little Jenni. I guess
you have played a big part in my life as well. I want you
to know, we are going to be all right. We are learning how
to be a family and getting better every day. The three of us
want to say thank you. You have brought joy back to this
old farm. Your compassion has changed us forever."

As folks began to leave for the night, I tried to ensure
everybody took something home with them. Even though
James and Little Jenni might have hoped I would save
some things and avoid sandwiches for a few days, I made
sure everybody took hamburgers, hot dogs, cookies, cake,
or something home with them. James brought buckets of
water from the creek to douse the fire, and then it was time
to walk the last of our guests to their car. As we walked
with Sheriff Joe, his wife, and his grandchildren, he turned
to me and said, "Will, for a good part of the evening, there
was something or someone at the top of the ridge watching.
When we leave, I am going to swing around to the south

and make a pass up there to see if I see anybody. Keep an eye out for tonight."

"Man, you really are never off duty. I can walk up there."

"No, I will drive by."

CHAPTER FOURTEEN

It was a warm, sunny Sunday afternoon. The kids and I had returned home after church and enjoyed our lunch-time meal. It was a nice day to walk along the creek and tell stories to James and Little Jenni. I explained to them that when I was a child, my family was very poor and our lives were hard. Even as small children, we had chores and things we were responsible for. I even took my first job away from the farm when I was only eleven years old. In the rare free time for play, we had to find creative ways to entertain ourselves. I told them that, just like when I was young, the farm was their playground and they were free to explore and create games and activities they enjoyed. I shared a story about when my brothers and I were younger and occasionally had boat races on the creek.

I began my story. "Many times over the years, when rain would cause the creek to rise and run a bit quicker, my brothers and I had boat races. Whatever we could find that would float, those objects became our boats. A small piece of Styrofoam or a piece of light wood was quickly transformed into our river-faring vessels."

It seemed they were somewhat amused by the story, so I continued. "We deployed the boats at our south fence and would race to the small bridge at the north end of the property. I guess it probably took a couple of hours to cover that distance. We each chose a good stick as our instrument to navigate our boats on their journey. We zigzagged our way down the creek, running, yelling, and laughing. It was so much fun." I told James and Little Jenni that we would have boat races later in the summer.

I also walked them to a location on the hillside where we had played as children. I told them, "During the winter months after the leaves had fallen from the trees, we would use a piece of cardboard to slide down the hill. You would be surprised by how fast you can go. You just have to make sure you do not land in the creek."

James asked, "Can we do it now?"

I told him, "If you want to run back to the barn and see if you can find a box or a piece of cardboard, we will try. The leaves are not as thick and dry as they are later in the winter, but we can try." I'm not sure I had ever seen them run as fast as they did to get back to the barn. A few minutes later, they returned with two boxes in hand. We unfolded the flaps of the boxes and made two "cardboard racers." We climbed to near the top of the hill. I placed James on his piece of cardboard, and with only a gentle push, he began sliding down the hill. He gathered speed as he neared the bottom of the hill and screamed. Little Jenni and I were laughing as James rolled from his cardboard racer before going into the creek.

I asked Little Jenni if she wanted to try. I explained that she may not weigh enough to go as fast as James. She said, "That is okay. I am scared." I reassured her she would be all right as she sat on her cardboard racer. As with James, I gave Little Jenni a gentle push and she began her downhill adventure. She did not go as fast as James but fast enough to satisfy the daredevil in her. She had not reached the bottom of the hill when she rolled off her cardboard racer and slid to a stop. They retrieved their cardboard racers and returned to the top of the hill. They were up and down the hill until their cardboard racers were tattered and torn. I explained that they were welcome to come back and play there anytime. I just needed to know where they were. I told them that maybe I would be able to join them someday.

Chapter Fifteen

It was a warm, quiet evening. The windows and the front door were open, allowing a bit of a breeze to blow through the house. We were relaxing and watching television when we heard a car coming up our road. James ran to the door and said, "It is Sheriff Joe."

"I wonder what he could want at this hour." I waited for Sheriff Joe to walk across the yard and met him on the front porch. "Good evening," I said as I reached to shake his hand.

"Good evening, Will." From the tone of his voice, I sensed this was not going to be something I wanted to hear. I had not noticed, but James and Little Jenni followed behind me and were anxious to see Sheriff Joe. As had become customary, he greeted them with a warm smile and a handshake. He knelt in front of them and asked, "James, Little Jenni, how would you like to be my deputies?"

They looked at each other with a surprised expression but said, "Can we be deputies?"

As Sheriff Joe retrieved two plastic badges from his pocket and handed them to James and Little Jenni, he told them, "Yes, you can be my deputies. If you see any strange characters around the farm, you call me. That is what my deputies do." He turned to me. "Take a walk with me, Will."

I told James and Little Jenni to finish watching their television show and I would be back in a few minutes. The sheriff and I did not say a word to each other as we walked across the yard, but when we got to his patrol car, he began to speak. "Will, we have another one."

I knew what that meant but could not stop myself from asking, "Another what?"

"Another homicide. Not just another homicide, but it is like Jenni. A farmer found the body just inside his fence line and called it in. Like Jenni, the body was found about a mile from the interstate highway. It was in Oklahoma, a few miles before the state line outside of Joplin, Missouri. Also like Jenni, the body had been burned. With it being similar to Jenni's murder, not only will the Oklahoma State Bureau of Investigation investigate, but the Federal Bureau of Investigation will be involved as well. Anytime it appears to be serial, the feds will be involved."

So many thoughts immediately raced through my mind. Was Jake being honest when he said he had nothing to do with Jenni's murder, or was he simply trying to deflect blame? What happens when the FBI reviews the investigation into the shooting of Jake Cummings by the deputies? What happens if they review the ballistics reports and see one bullet that does not match either deputy's service weapon? I realized the possibility that an investigation by the OSBI and the FBI would lead to numerous questions about Sheriff Joe, and his deputies, and the idea that they may have ignored evidence to prevent an investigation into a possible shooting by a citizen. But probably my greatest concern at that moment was not knowing how much I could ask Sheriff Joe or disclose to him. He had never asked, and I had never disclosed to him the details of the night Jake Cummings died.

I assumed it would take weeks for the OSBI and the FBI to mobilize and get resources there, but to my surprise, they moved into the county courthouse quickly and began their investigation within a few days. Each organization committed two to three agents on the ground, and I assumed additional agents supported the investigation from their headquarters.

A few weeks into their investigation, it occurred to me that Sheriff Joe had not stopped by the house for one of what had become his frequent visits. I had to assume that his absence was intentional, but why? Maybe I was being investigated and he had to maintain his distance and not have contact with me. Maybe he was afraid that a visit could lead to a discussion of things he could not share or did not want to hear. I had been nervous since Sheriff Joe told me there would be an investigation, but I was beginning to become concerned. I was not inclined to share details of that night, but I wanted to learn any details of the investigation that could be shared. I decided to visit CPS to provide an impromptu update on James and Little Jenni. Maybe I would bump into Sheriff Joe and we would have a chance to speak.

I took a few minutes to clean up and then drove to the courthouse. I assumed if I did see Sheriff Joe, his facial expression would tell me whether he was available to speak. I lingered in the hallway for a moment, but not seeing him, I opened the door and went into the CPS offices. I walked to the counter and asked whether Shelley Corntassel was available. From a back room, a voice asked, "Is that William Rogers I hear?"

The young lady at the counter replied, "Yes it is."

Shelley Corntassel exited her office, walked through the swinging gate doors, and extended her arms, seeking an embrace. I hugged Shelley and told her, "I thought I would stop by and let you know the kids and I are doing well. Amy is with them today, running errands and doing some shopping for them." We shared some small talk for a few minutes, and I told Shelley it was great to see her and to feel free to stop by and visit with James and Little Jenni. We would always welcome her visit.

Like before, as I left CPS, I lingered for a moment in the hallway. As I was walking toward the door to leave the courthouse, I heard Sheriff Joe talking as he left his office. I turned back to the hallway and caught his eye. He yelled down the hallway, "Hey, Will. Hang on a second." As he approached, he said, "I have been wanting to speak with you for a few days now, but with this investigation going on, I have just not had the time."

I said, "I noticed I had not seen you for some weeks now but assumed you were busy."

At this point, we were walking toward the exit doors, and he asked, "Do you have time to grab lunch? If so, meet me at Penney's Café across the street and we can talk. I have one quick stop to make, and I will meet you there. I need to share some things with you."

I immediately understood that if he had things he could share with me, I was probably not being investigated. At least I hoped I was not being investigated. That aroused some hope and relief in me. I told him, "I will see you there in a few minutes."

It was late morning and a little while ahead of the lunch rush, so we were able to find a quiet corner table where we could speak. He began, "First, let me say, sometimes things just need to be left alone to be forgotten. So I never discussed with you our investigation into the night Jake died, my deputies' involvement in that, and especially your possible involvement in that. When we examined ballistics reports on the bullets recovered from that night, the reports were clear there were no bullets fired from your gun, only my deputies' service weapons. Jake sustained one wound, a through-and-through, that we never found a bullet for. We left that with the assumption it was a wound from a deputy. There was no reason to believe otherwise. The number of bullets accounted for plus the one missing round equaled the number of times the deputies' weapons were fired."

I quickly understood that one of the deputies, in the excitement of the moment, must have fired a round that did not hit Jake or his vehicle. It was simply a wild shot.

Sheriff Joe continued. "Will, it looks like you are free from this. The OSBI and the FBI have completed their investigation here and are moving to Joplin and will continue their investigation there. There have been two agents investigating the homicide there since the body was found. Now they will combine forces and continue their investigation. They have been through our investigation of Jenni's homicide and our internal investigation into the night Jake died at the hands of my deputies. At one point, they inquired about interviewing you, but they decided to use your previous statements and our files. They told us that if your previous statements were not sufficient, they would call you in to be interviewed. They did interview Josh and Amy to confirm your arrival time that evening. They knew what time it was when you drove past Longhorn Ranch, and once Josh and Amy confirmed your arrival time at their house, they removed you from their list of possible suspects. If Josh and Amy have not disclosed the interview to you, do not hold it against them. They were told not to discuss it with you.

"Regarding Jake, like us, they investigated every move my deputies made from the time the county dispatcher logged the call from your neighbor to the findings from Jake's autopsy. Although the gunshots your neighbor reported have never been explained, the shooting by my deputies was ruled as justified. I have suspected from the beginning of their investigation that they were also looking at me and my office, and our investigation. I was not worried about that. I had seen all the evidence they were going to see. I knew all was well.

"The OSBI and FBI will hold a brief press conference where they will discuss the two cases. Their statement will be that the recent homicide appears to be related, but they have not ruled out that it is a copycat crime. Until they complete their investigation of the second homicide, there is not enough evidence to make a confident decision either way, but I believe they like Jake for Jenni's murder. I would say they are leaning toward it being a copycat."

He looked across the table at me and said, "Will, what you did that night in self-defense will always be self-defense. That does not change. We know Jake was at your place, and we know he was armed. So, if it became necessary to defend yourself, it was justified in the eyes of the law. If you discharged your weapon in self-defense, you are good. There is no evidence that you shot Jake. That will not change."

I interrupted him and said, "But, Sheriff, Jake said he did not hurt Jenni."

He said, "Will, you cannot let the doubt about Jake's guilt and what happened to him that night fester in your mind. It will eat you alive. You must separate emotion from 'law.' Emotion does not apply. Laws exist to protect us from danger and harm. Whether you and Jake had history, or whether he was a suspect in Jenni's murder, when he came to your house, armed with a firearm, he became subject to a law that allows you to defend yourself. When he refused to disarm himself and surrender to my deputies, he became subject to a law that allowed my deputies to protect themselves, thereby removing a danger or a risk. Jake was not shot because he was a suspect. We have no law that allows us to shoot someone because they are suspected of a crime.

"One last thing, Will. After the hayride at your farm, I did circle back to the south of your place as we discussed. I found the spot where I had seen the person watching us. I found two cigarette butts and submitted them for DNA testing. The results came back for a guy named Terry Ralston. Does that name mean anything to you?"

"No, the name does not ring a bell."

"He is from the Joplin area and did a stint in the Missouri State Penitentiary up in Springfield for a very violent assault and attempted murder. He was released in May of last year."

"That name does not sound familiar to me. If something comes to me, I will let you know. Thank you, Sheriff."

"Like I told you before, if you ever need anything, I will stand beside you. Again, it looks like you are free from this. You can focus your attention on James and Little Jenni. Let's get some lunch."

I smiled and said, "Thank you, Sheriff. What do you usually get when you are here?"

"I recommend the chicken-fried steak."

CHAPTER SIXTEEN

The homicide near Joplin, Missouri, occurred on May 5, 2011. In the early morning of May 17, agents from the FBI knocked on my door and advised that I needed to appear at the Fain County Sheriff's office the following morning at 8:00 a.m. to be interviewed regarding the recent homicide. They said I should clear my calendar for the morning and plan to be there until at least lunchtime. As I guess should be expected, there was no real small talk, only a couple of brief comments about how nice the farm looked. They asked if the two children were home. I advised that it was a school day and they would be out for the summer the following week. As they began their walk toward their vehicle, one of the agents turned and handed me a business card as he said, "If you have any questions between now and tomorrow, feel free to call."

It did not take long after their departure for me to call Sheriff Joe. As he answered my call, he immediately said, "Will, you should be expecting a call or visit from the FBI."

"They just left my house. What am I up against, Sheriff?"

"As long as you did nothing, you should be fine. If you are meeting in Fain County, this is about the murder up there. Just remember, you do not have to do the interview without an attorney. But I do not think you need one for this interview. Just be honest, direct, and brief with your responses. I don't quite understand at this point why they want to interview you for that case. I assume that will be brought to light soon enough. I would not expect it, but they may throw in some questions about Jake. Do not be surprised if they do. The last thing, Will, your interview will not be like coming to my office and talking to me. It will be very formal and long. They will repeat questions with slight variations in their wording just to check the consistency of your answers. They will record your interview. Do not worry, you will be fine."

My drive home was occupied with so many thoughts and questions about what the next day would bring. Although I knew I had been nowhere near Joplin recently, I could not help being concerned that I was about to be interviewed by the FBI. What could have been a normal routine morning for me was now filled with anxiety and a feeling that I needed to rush through my morning to get to my interview on time. My daily schedule is dictated by routine. It is not commonplace for me to have assigned times to be somewhere. I rushed through breakfast and hardly ate a bite. I just shuffled things around on my plate. I rushed through town and turned north toward Fain County. I arrived twenty minutes early and sat in my truck fidgeting and waiting for the top of the hour. A couple minutes before eight, I gathered myself and entered the courthouse. Having spent a night or two in the drunk tank there, I remembered where the sheriff's office was located.

The two FBI agents who had visited the farm met me in the lobby and escorted me to an interview room. Having seen interrogation rooms on television, I was not surprised by the appearance of the room. Other than one table, four chairs, and a video camera, the room was empty. I do not know what the temperature was in the room, but the atmosphere was cold. I had never thought about it while watching police dramas on television, but I now assumed there was a reason the room was empty, eliminating anything for suspects to focus on during their time there, driving home the fact that they are alone.

Agent Lewis was a taller, thin, blonde-haired man, probably six feet, one inch tall. Agent Jorgenson was probably five feet, eight inches tall but a bit stockier than Agent Lewis. Things were cordial but extremely businesslike. The agents set a bottle of water in front of me and explained the interview process, saying that they would be present, along with a person taking notes, and the video camera would be on for the duration of my interview. They did not introduce the third person in the room. Before taking his seat, Agent Lewis turned on the video camera and said, "Will, you are allowed to have an attorney present, if you prefer."

"I am fine without one. I have committed no crime, but I will keep that in mind if it should become necessary." Once the formalities of my name, age, and address were taken care of, the interview began.

The first question was a complete surprise to me. While Agent Jorgenson sat back in his chair, Agent Lewis leaned forward, placing his elbows on the table. He looked straight into my eyes and asked, "What was your relationship with Jenni Whittington?"

"She was a friend," I said.

Quickly, Agent Lewis asked, "Were you ever more than friends?"

I answered, "Yes, sir."

"Describe the time that you were more than friends, and the nature of your relationship," Agent Lewis directed.

I described the years that Jenni and I had dated during high school and college. I added that, since her marriage to Scott Barro, we had gone through a period of friendship. I also mentioned that, after Scott died, I occasionally visited to help Jenni whenever and however I could.

Agent Jorgenson had remained quiet for the first few minutes of the interview but now asked, "You were only friends? Is it true that one of her children is your son?"

I said, "I was never told that by Jenni in person, but from information provided by Sheriff Robertson, I believe that is true."

"If you were only friends at the time she was with Mr. Barro, how did you have a child with her?"

I stammered for a second while I searched for an answer. "That was a one-time thing. We met one night before they were married and let ourselves get carried away. Outside of that night, we remained friends." I asked, "May I ask a question?"

Agent Jorgenson replied an affirmative with a nod of his head.

"Understand, I am willing to sit here and answer your questions because I know I have done nothing wrong, but why do we need to cover ground that you already know the answers to? Please do not think I am being uncooperative or combative, but I see no reason to cover old territory." Up to that point, I had wondered why there was a third person in the room. For me, their reaction to my question provided an answer. They were there to observe me, not take notes of the interview.

Agent Lewis leaned forward. "This may be cliché, but we will ask the questions. If the most recent case is related to the Jenni Whittington murder, we want to get your background story. Where were you on the evening that Jenni Whittington was murdered?"

"I was on Route 66, en route to some friends' house for dinner. And of course, I was at their house for dinner," I answered.

Agent Jorgenson asked, "Did you note anything odd or out of the ordinary during your drive?"

"Yes. I observed a man standing behind a vehicle partially pulled onto the shoulder of the highway."

"What was the man doing?" asked Jorgenson.

Trying to mask my frustration, I answered, "I do not know what he was doing."

"Was that the location of Jenni's murder?" asked Agent Lewis.

I said, "I actually do not know the exact location where Jenni's body was discovered. So I do not know the answer to that question."

"Was it near Farm Road 71?" Agent Lewis asked.

"Yes."

From there, we moved to questions about Jake Cummings. It was more of the same, questions they already knew the answer to from statements I had provided to Sheriff Joe and the Carlin County district attorney. We were well past an hour into the interview when they asked if I would like to take a fifteen-minute break. I replied that I did need to use the restroom but five minutes would be sufficient for me.

It took the agents the full fifteen minutes to return to the table and continue their questions. In retrospect, I assume their slow return was intentional. They had been asking questions they knew I would be relatively comfortable answering. Giving me the full fifteen minutes gave me time to anticipate additional questions about Jake and Jenni.

Agent Lewis, now sitting back in his chair, asked, "Do you know Laura Smith?"

I said, "Yes, I know a Laura Smith. What does she have to do with the homicide?"

Agent Jorgenson looked into my eyes. "She is the second victim. What was your relationship with her?"

My mind raced with many questions, and I could feel my body reacting nervously. The person taking notes was busy writing. I asked, "Are you sure it was Laura Smith?"

"Yes," Agent Jorgenson said.

I said, "I was briefly married to a Laura Smith. Is it the same Laura Smith?"

"Yes, it is the Laura Smith who previously lived off of West Seventh Street in Joplin that you married and divorced," Agent Jorgenson said.

"When was the last time you saw her?" asked Agent Lewis.

I was now getting alternating rapid-fire questions from both agents. "I saw her and we spoke briefly about a year ago at a restaurant in Joplin, but I have not seen her since," I answered.

"You have not seen her since the time at the restaurant?" Jorgenson asked.

"I just answered that."

"Will, do you know a man named Terry Ralston?" Agent Lewis asked.

I was probably squirming in my chair at this point. I knew that name from Sheriff Joe and did not want to give any indication that he had shared information related to the case with me. I had made a great effort to maintain eye contact with the agents up to this point, but I caught myself beginning to look around the room for something to focus on other than them. I was ignoring the note-taker. I am sure they were writing furiously as I looked for some type of comfort. "I do not know Terry Ralston," I said.

Agent Jorgenson said, "Will, tell us about your relationship with Laura."

I do not know why I decided at that time to start telling stories, but I started talking. "I met her at a bar in Joplin in 2004. We . . . I cannot really say dated, but we spent some time together in various bars, thought we were in love, and decided to get married. After my first wife divorced me and moved my kids to California, I became a bit of a barfly. I had an empty place in my life and was looking for someone to fill it. I did not realize that when a relationship is developed through an alcohol-soaked period, things will probably not end well. If the only times you spend together involve alcohol, you do not truly know who that person is when you get sober. About six months into our marriage, I got sober, and she did not. Suddenly she found herself with a man she did not know. The drunk Will was a lot more fun than the sober Will. I found myself with someone who did not share my desire to get back to life and work my farm. We ended our relationship and were divorced in less than eighteen months, in 2006. Like I said, since that time, I have seen her once during a chance encounter at a restaurant in Joplin."

Agent Lewis asked, "Will, you do not know Terry Ralston?"

"No, sir."

He continued. "Did Laura know Terry Ralston? Was he somebody she dated?"

"I have no idea who she knew or dated after we divorced. If she knew him, she never mentioned him to me," I explained.

Agent Jorgenson asked, "Will, where were you on May 5?"

"I don't necessarily remember May 5 exactly, but I am sure I was working at the farm, and then home with the kids. No, wait a second, May 5, I picked up a day of work for a friend doing a small remodel job at a house on the lake. Since I was in town, when school let out, I picked up the kids and drove them home."

"Who did you do the remodel work for?" Agent Jorgenson asked.

"Lee Wilson. He runs a carpentry business in town. After we finish, I can get his number from my phone if you would like."

Agent Jorgenson smiled a dry smile and said, "We can get his number."

They explained that they would verify all the information I shared and, if necessary, let me know if they had additional questions for me. I explained they were welcome to call me anytime but sometimes, when I was on the tractor, I missed calls. They should just leave a message and I would return their call. With that, the interview ended. We were finished in time for me to grab an early lunch at my favorite burger place in town before making the drive home. Even when I picked up my order from the counter and sat down, my hands were still a bit shaky.

As I started my drive home, I called Sheriff Joe's office to schedule a meeting. Like on my drive home the previous day, the barrage of questions by Agents Lewis and Jorgenson ran through my mind. I kept thinking of the things I wished I had said. But I was so thankful that I had remembered working the remodel job with Lee Wilson. Sheriff Joe commented that his schedule had been abnormally busy but asked if I could come by his office a couple of days later. He instructed me to call Beverly to set up a time. Following the call with Beverly, I called the attorney's office and scheduled a meeting with Bruce to follow my meeting with Sheriff Joe.

CHAPTER SEVENTEEN

My appointment was scheduled with Sheriff Joe at eleven o'clock at Penney's Café. I was anxious to tell him about my interview with the FBI and to listen to anything he might be able to share. Since I was a few minutes early, I decided to stop by his office, assuming we would walk over to Penney's together. As I walked through the door to the sheriff's office, Beverly looked up and saw me. She said, "He is not busy. Go on in."

I approached his door, thanked Beverly, and knocked.

"Come on in," he said. "Will, it is good to see you. How are my two favorite kids doing?"

"They are well, Sheriff. They have just about worn the finish off the badges you gave them. I think I am going to have to buy them their own patrol car soon," I said as we laughed.

"Have a seat and let's catch up, Will. I know you had your interview with the FBI, but I have not heard much beyond that. Even the sheriff up in Fain County is not hearing too much from the FBI. Like everybody else in the area, I saw the press release that the victim up there was Laura Smith. Is that the lady you were married to for a couple of years?"

I nodded to acknowledge it was the Laura Smith I had been briefly married to.

He looked across his desk at me. "Your situation has been a tangled mess since this started. From the time Russell was married to Jenni, I liked her. She was a special young lady, and she held a special place in my heart. Then she was murdered and, while we were taking a long hard look at you, we learned that one of her children is your child. That just made things murkier. Then you take in her children. Now your ex-wife is the victim in a second homicide. This is hands down the most twisted case I have ever been involved in. But when you stood up for those kids, I told myself you are still the man I knew years ago, a man who will fight for what he believes is right."

"Sheriff, are we allowed to talk about the investigation into the second homicide? I do not want to do something that could cause problems for you."

He explained, "If we get into territory we cannot cover, I will let you know. But, at this point, I do not think I even know any details that would be out of bounds. Before we continue, I want to finish what I was saying. In the years that Jenni was married to my deadbeat nephew, you were not her only advocate. Will, I fought with my entire family trying to clean that up and get her out of that marriage. You never realized what I was doing behind the scenes. I was the one who pushed to get charges filed against him when he slapped her in that restaurant. That is the end of that discussion. Now, tell me about your interview."

I said, "They began with questions about Jenni and Jake. It was a bit of a surprise, but they were all softball questions. I do not think there was anything I have not said on the record previously. It took a while for me to understand, but I think the third person, whom they never introduced, was there to watch me and take notes about my reaction to their questions, not my actual responses. We took a brief break, and when we reconvened, they hit me with Laura Smith's name. They followed that with Terry Ralston. Having begun the interview with questions about Jenni and Jake, they definitely caught me off guard with those questions. I became very uncomfortable, and I am sure it was evident. I thought about stopping the interview and getting Bruce involved, but I think it was all right. They had told me to expect the interview to take all morning and to clear my calendar for the whole day, but we were finished in just over two hours. As we finished, I told them to feel free to call me anytime if they had additional questions. I thought I would offer since they will contact me anyway. Sheriff Joe, I hope you can give me some insight into what is going on. It cannot be a coincidence that this has happened to two women who had been close to me. And have you learned any details about this Terry Ralston guy?"

"First, if it only lasted a couple of hours or so, that is probably a good thing. Were you able to account for your whereabouts on May 5?"

"Yes, I was doing a remodel job with Lee Wilson, and then picked up the kids at school."

"That is good. As soon as they can verify that with Lee and verify you were at the school picking up the kids, that should get them to back off you a bit. But even with that, the victim being your ex-wife will keep you in their sights for a while. I strongly suspect Terry Ralston is the answer to this case. The question I cannot answer is why he would have been at your farm the evening of the hayride. You are sure you do not know Terry Ralston?"

I told him again, "I do not know him. Unless he was some guy I met in a bar back in my drinking days and have forgotten his name, I do not know him."

"I have provided a statement from the evening of the hayride and the DNA reports for Terry Ralston to the FBI. It will be up to them to find a connection between him and Laura if there is a connection. If he was involved in Laura's death somehow, he would almost have to be the one who killed Jenni. It defies the odds that two identical homicides involving women close to you would be committed by two different men. The only way that would have happened is if Ralston knew Jake, and only Ralston can tell us that at this point. My office took a look into whether they knew each other for the last week or so, and we cannot find that they ever served time together. If they knew each other, it would have been from a time outside of prison. The FBI has a lot of resources. They will find out how Ralston fits into this. He either knows you, knew Jake, or knew Laura Smith. But I am telling you, he is the key to this. If I hear that the FBI has found him, I will let you know."

"You think he is involved?" I asked.

"If he had not been at your farm watching you, I would say he might or might not be, but that one simple fact says he is in the middle of it. I am sure of that." With that, he reached into his pocket and retrieved a photo. "I almost forgot to give you this. It is a picture of Terry Ralston. If you see him, call me. Unless he makes a life-threatening gesture toward you, please do not shoot him," he remarked with a bit of a sideways grin.

I looked at the picture. "He is an ordinary-looking guy. You would never suspect him of a violent crime by looking at him. Sheriff, since we intended to meet at Penney's, and if you are hungry, I'll buy lunch."

He patted himself on the stomach. "I try not to miss any meals, especially free ones. Let's go."

CHAPTER EIGHTEEN

As the sheriff and I took our seats at Penney's Café, I gazed around the room at the many high school and college sports teams signs, posters, and pictures. As I was scanning the room, I saw Bruce sipping on a tall glass of iced tea. I walked over, shook his hand, and commented about the artwork on the walls. I chuckled and said that he was sitting by the only University of Tulsa poster in the entire café.

He said, "I will always be proud to have been on the faculty at the University of Tulsa. That is why Penney has this one lone poster."

I told him I would be by his office after lunch. "I think we have a one o'clock appointment."

"I will see you then."

Shelley Corntassel's comment that Jenni may have been thinking we could have a relationship in the future had haunted me for all these months. I might have never thought we would be a couple again but now acknowledged that I would have welcomed it if she had wanted that. Now knowing that James was my son made the likelihood we could have gotten back together even greater. It was a hard feeling to understand and accept, but I felt I had lost a close family member, not just a girlfriend from my teenage years. I now understood that I still had a special place in Jenni's heart, like she had in mine. We had gone through our entire relationship without being intimate and then shared one passionate night at Cain's Bayou. I realized she wanted to experience that with me before committing the rest of her life to Scott. I know, for Jenni, that was the ultimate expression of love. It was not something she would have done without thinking it through.

Understanding there was some possibility we could have become a family when Jenni was alive, I decided it was time to proceed with investigating adopting James and Little Jenni. It had been almost one year since Jenni was murdered and eight months since I had gotten custody of the kids.

After lunch with the sheriff, I headed to the law office. At one o'clock sharp, the receptionist looked at me and said, "Will, Bruce is available. You may go back to his office."

I thanked her and made my way down the hall to his office. A lot of water had passed under the bridge since Bruce and I last met face-to-face. But, true to his word, he had been actively managing Jenni's estate and ensuring her farm was secured for James and Little Jenni. As anybody who knew Bruce would expect, he greeted me at his office door with a handshake and a warm, welcoming smile.

Years prior during a visit, I had commented to Bruce that he always seemed upbeat and happy, telling him, "Everybody deals with issues and hardships, but you always seem to be in a good place. If you could package and sell that, you would be a rich man." He'd chuckled at my observation and said, "Will, trust me, I have hard times in my life like everybody else. But I handle so many estates and probate cases, I understand that my clients are typically going through some of the hardest times in their lives. I try to remain positive and welcoming. I hope that will take away some of the stress, pain, and uncertainty of those times for them."

As I walked through his door now, Bruce asked, "Will, how are the kids?"

"They are adapting well. You know how resilient children can be. We have made it through the holidays, a semester of school, and two birthday parties. James is now eight and Little Jenni is six."

"That all sounds positive."

"I think it has been as good as anyone could ever expect. I appreciate all the work you have done with probate on Jenni's case and her estate. I definitely appreciate the payment terms. That will allow me to pay your fees without needing to sell any of our cattle. Bruce, I will never be able to make that up to you."

"That is not a big deal. A lot of folks around here have taken note of what you are doing for James and Little Jenni. You can count me as one of your fans for what you are doing. If our arrangement helps you, I am happy to help."

"Thank you. That means a lot. Jenni's farm is looking good. This year's crops are in the ground and starting to come up. If we can get an occasional rain, we should have a great crop this year. Like I mentioned last year, I would like to adopt the kids."

"Have you discussed adoption with James and Little Jenni?" he asked.

"No, but I plan to speak with them when they get home from school today. I have no idea what the adoption process entails, or what preliminary work may need to be done."

"Will, like most folks in the area, I am aware of the homicide up in Fain County and assume, since the victim was one of your ex-wives, the FBI has some interest in you. That is an issue. Considering the ongoing investigation into that case, it would be best if we waited to file for the adoption of the kids."

"Bruce, I had no involvement in Laura's death, but yes, they have interviewed me, and they should know by now I was nowhere near Joplin that day and have a rock-solid alibi to prove it."

"I have no doubt about your innocence. I am just letting you know we need to let the investigation progress for a while before we file papers for adoption. But I will begin the process of documenting your case for adoption. That way, when the time is right to file, you will be ready, and we will hopefully be able to move the case through the system a bit quicker than usual."

I rose from my chair. "Thank you. I am sure you have other business to take care of. Bruce, as always, it has been a pleasure. If I hear anything from the FBI, I will let you know."

When I was anywhere near the courthouse, a quick visit to CPS was a must for me. So I entered and asked if Shelley was available, just as she walked through the door behind me. I asked whether she had a few minutes to talk.

She said, "Come back to my office." As we entered her office, she closed the door behind us. "Will, I am glad you stopped by. I was going to call you this afternoon. The homicide and investigation in Fain County are beginning to concern us. I have spoken with Sheriff Joe, and I one hundred percent believe you had nothing to do with the murder, but if the FBI considers you a suspect, we will have to look at removing James and Little Jenni from your custody."

I said, "They are doing so well. You cannot do that to them. You cannot start yanking them back and forth. For heaven's sake, I just spoke with Bruce about moving forward with adoption. That is not right. I have done nothing wrong, and those kids have done nothing wrong. You cannot punish them for something they are not involved in. I am trying to do right by James and Little Jenni. I am trying to give them stability and security. You cannot take them away."

"Will, you know it is not what I want, but we are required to do certain things under certain conditions. So we will be watching the investigation and checking in with Sheriff Joe, and the FBI."

"Well, if you decide to take them, please do not just show up at the door. Give me some warning so I can talk to the kids about it before you get there."

When I arrived home, I could see a black sedan in my driveway. I was sure I recognized the vehicle. Indeed, it was Agents Jorgenson and Lewis.

Agent Jorgenson started the conversation by saying they wanted to interview the children.

I said, "I am sure you know better than I do, but of course an adult will have to be present, and I assume since they are still wards of the state, I figure CPS will want to be present or have a legal representative there. If they assign someone to be present, I will make myself scarce."

Agent Lewis said, "Yes, CPS will be responsible for appearing with the children. We have scheduled with them, and you will need to make the children available. Due to your position in the investigation, you will not be present."

I had been understanding of their position and how things may have looked for me, but my patience was beginning to wear thin. I said, "Gentlemen, you have had an opportunity to check my alibi and run down any existing video around town to verify I was nowhere near Joplin on May 5. And you surely understand I am in no way involved in Laura's murder. I need you to step up and admit that I am not involved before CPS does something ridiculous and turns those kids' world upside down again. I have fought my demons over the years and may not have always been the victor, but I am still standing upright and have an opportunity to do what I believe is right. I am trying to do right by those kids."

Agent Lewis's reply was brief. "Please make the children available at one o'clock tomorrow afternoon. Thank you."

They got in their vehicle and drove away. I stood and watched until the car disappeared around the turn in the road at the north end of the valley.

As soon as the kids got off the school bus, I asked them to have a seat at the kitchen table, as I needed to ask them a question. I found myself slightly nervous. "You have been living with me on the farm for eight months now. I love both of you and love having you live with me. If you will have me, I would like to make that permanent."

With a look of innocence that only Little Jenni possessed, she gazed up at me and asked, "What does that mean?"

I said, "What that means is, I would like to adopt you. I think we are a family now, but that would make us a family legally. Would you like that?"

James said, "Yes, I would like that."

Little Jenni, still a bit puzzled by the concept, said, "I thought we were already a family."

I explained, "We are a family, and that will not change. Adoption just makes it legal and permanent. If you want, you can even change your last name to my last name. I asked an attorney today if he would help us get through the adoption process. Also, there has been an issue come up, and some gentlemen from the FBI would like to ask you some questions. So, tomorrow, I will pick you up early from school and we will go see Mrs. Corntassel at CPS."

"What is FBI?" Little Jenni asked.

"They are lawmen, like Sheriff Joe. They just do not wear a cool cowboy hat like Sheriff Joe does."

As directed by Agents Jorgenson and Lewis, the following day, I delivered James and Little Jenni to CPS for their interview. As soon as we entered the office, Shelley Corntassel hustled the kids to a back room, and I left. Not wanting to be anywhere near the courthouse, I drove south and located a nice shade tree in the state park. This park had a couple of the many spillways used to help maintain the lake water level. It was relaxing to sit and listen to the water as it cascaded over the top of the spillway and crashed into the pools below. I knew this would be a good way for me to spend the two hours I was instructed to be away from the courthouse.

Shelley had told me that if the interview finished earlier than the scheduled two hours, she would call me. True to her word, as I sat and listened to the water running over the spillway, she called. It was about fifteen minutes before three o'clock, and she said the interview was complete and I could pick up James and Little Jenni.

When I arrived at the courthouse, Shelley was outside with the kids, and I did not even need to get out of my truck. She walked them to me, and we drove away. It was a quiet drive home other than a little small talk about their friends from school. I did not want to put them in the hard position of answering questions for me, so we never discussed the interview and what was asked and said that afternoon.

CHAPTER NINETEEN

A couple mornings later, Agents Jorgenson and Lewis called. Agent Lewis said, "Will, we need to discuss the Laura Smith case with you. We have had some developments since we interviewed the children. Are you able to meet us at Sheriff Robertson's office at, let's say, one o'clock this afternoon?"

I said, "Yes, I will meet you there at one o'clock."

I arrived at the sheriff's office a couple of minutes before one o'clock. As I entered the office, Beverly looked up from her computer and said, "Go on in, Will. They are waiting for you."

I am normally a relatively calm guy, but I guess my anxiety was showing. Beverly looked at me and, in a comforting tone, said, "Will, it is okay."

"Thanks, Beverly," I said.

Immediately, I noticed the atmosphere seemed a bit different. Sheriff Joe seemed to be in a more casual mood. Even the agents seemed less rigid than before. Sheriff Joe was the first to greet me. As he rose from his chair and reached across his desk to shake my hand, he said, "Will, come on in here."

Agents Jorgenson and Lewis did the same. "Have a seat, Will," Agent Lewis instructed. "We have had a break in the Laura Smith case. Actually, a federal prosecutor is in the process of filing charges as we speak. We are charging Terry Ralston with the murder of Jenni Whittington and Laura Smith. Let me catch you up on the details. Several days ago, Shelley Corntassel, in a conversation with Sheriff Robertson, informed him that she had been in contact with us regarding the status of the children and their current custody situation. Sheriff Robertson, understanding the implications and not wanting to see a disruption in the lives of the children, doubled down his department's efforts to find a connection between Jake Cummings, Terry Ralston, and Laura Smith. On nothing more than a gut feeling, the sheriff and his deputies began reviewing the Longhorn Ranch security video again. Of course, when they reviewed the video previously, they would not necessarily have known who Terry Ralston and Laura Smith were. Now that they have photos of them, they quickly realized they were both at the Longhorn Ranch convenience store at the same time as Jenni Whittington. We were already trying to find a connection between Ralston and Laura and had spoken with numerous individuals who had disclosed a romantic relationship between them. But when we inter-viewed Ralston, he denied knowing Laura Smith. So, since we knew there was a relationship, we knew he was being dishonest. When we showed Ralston the security video, he knew he was cornered. It was not long after that he began to speak. He walked us through all the details."

I doubt it is customary to let a previous suspect read another person's confession, but Sheriff Joe handed me a copy of the transcript of Ralston's confession. As he reached out to hand me the transcript, he said, "Will, I know what Jenni meant to you. This is hard to read."

"Thank you." I knew I had to learn the answers to the questions that had haunted me for all these months. I began reading the confession of Terry Ralston.

Laura Smith and I were enjoying a drive along Route 66 and were passing through the Longhorn Ranch area. We stopped at the convenience store to get a couple fountain drinks and a snack. Laura recognized a lady she called Jenni in the store and told me to watch her while she waited in line to pay for our snacks. I saw this Jenni lady exit the store and walk toward the rear of the store. I motioned to Laura that I would be in the back of the store when she was finished. As I was moving the car to the small parking area at the rear of the store, Laura exited the building and met me. I found it quite odd, but she sat in the back seat of the car. We saw Jenni talking through a car window to some guy in a small light-blue sedan. He was a rough-looking character, but she seemed to know him. When he drove away, Laura called Jenni over to the car and introduced herself. After several minutes talking about Will, Laura asked whether she needed a ride, and offered to provide it. Laura had really played it up that she was still friendly with Will. Trying to gain her trust, you know? She accepted our offer of a ride and got into the back seat. We were barely out of the parking lot when Laura punched the lady in the throat. As she leaned forward and grabbed her throat, Laura hit her with a tire tool that was in the back floorboard. The lady fell against the back of the seat and the passenger-side window. Laura, with her knees now in the seat, punched her in the face multiple times. The lady was limp. She put up no defense at all. I assumed she was dead from the blow to the head. The first road we came to, I dragged her body into a field. Laura had gotten a gas can out of the trunk and told me to pour the gas on her. I poured probably more than a half-gallon of gas on the lady, when Laura pulled a handful of dried grass from the ground, lit it, and threw it on her. We drove away without a word. I knew Laura did not like the lady because of her relationship with Will, but I have never seen that level of anger and hatred toward a person. We were never an ideal couple. You know, all couples have their disagreements and fights, but we had more than our share.

Laura had slapped and punched me on occasion, but I had no idea she was capable of that level of violence. We did not talk about that day again until the beginning of May. We had been fighting for several days when Laura threatened to go to the police and say that I had killed that lady. I ignored it as an idle threat for a couple of days, but she persisted. On the evening of May 4, we were arguing, and she slapped me. I pushed her away, but she charged me again, slapping and punching me multiple times. At some point, I lost it. I knocked her to the floor. She must have hit her head or something. She never woke up. I left her lying on the floor through the night and most of the following day. I had several hours to plan for what to do with her body. Even though I knew they had a suspect in that lady's homicide, I decided if I made it look like the earlier homicide, since Will Rogers knew both of them, he would most likely become the number-one suspect. I took her to a remote area, put her body in a field, poured gasoline on her, and burned her body.

The statement was signed and dated by Terry J. Ralston. I had not felt such an emotional gut punch since my parents died. Without speaking, I walked out of the sheriff's office and out the door of the courthouse. The images from that confession made me nauseous. I sat on the steps for several minutes before returning to Sheriff Joe's office.

As I walked in, Agent Jorgenson said, "We asked whether Jake Cummings was involved. Ralston said he did not know anybody by that name. We explained to him that Jake was at Longhorn Ranch and was leaving the store as he was entering. We explained that we think he was the man in the sedan he saw speaking with Jenni Whittington. He again denied knowing Jake Cummings. He added one additional detail though. Ralston claimed that as they were approaching Farm Road 71, a car that looked like the one from the store was pulling back onto the highway headed north. Our best guess is, the gas can Jake Cummings placed in his trunk had turned over and spilled. He was simply setting the can back upright when you passed. That was the gasoline odor you smelled. Also, we questioned Ralston but never received an explanation for why he was at your farm.

"Regarding the interview with the children, the kids' statements supported your story. James remembered you were late picking them up at school. He met Little Jenni and walked to their pickup spot and had to wait. He remembers that day because you took them to Walmart to get a treat because they had both been recognized at school as students of the week for their classes. We quickly realized Walmart's security video would verify James's statement. Although at this point it is of no consequence, Walmart's security video did support James's statement."

"So I am not a suspect?" I asked.

"No, sir. The books on this case will be closed soon. Terry Ralston's confession lines up with everything we know about each case," said Agent Lewis.

I said, "Gentlemen, you might call it a bribe, but be what it may, come what may. I will give anything I own to ensure those details are never made public. James and Little Jenni can never hear those details about their mother's death."

Agent Lewis said, "Will, we will do everything we can to prevent the details from being made public. As long as Ralston does not recant his confession and force us to disclose it during a trial, I think it will be all right. One last thing, Will, you should thank Sheriff Robertson for having the gut instinct to go back to the security video again. That was the one breakthrough we needed to solve both cases."

"Yes, I know I owe him a great debt," I said as I gave Sheriff Joe a hearty handshake. I asked whether the agents were finished with our meeting, thanked them again, and shook their hands. "I need to find Shelley Corntassel," I said as I rose from my chair to leave.

"Just a second, Will. If she is in the office, please tell her we will be there in a few minutes to wrap things up with her," Agent Lewis said.

Shelley was not in the office that afternoon, but I left a message that I was not a suspect in Laura Smith's murder and that I was going to move forward with adopting James and Little Jenni. I told the lady at the front desk that the FBI would stop by as well.

When I left CPS, I immediately walked across the street to Bruce's office. As we had discussed earlier, Bruce had been preparing my case for adopting James and Little Jenni. I apologized for appearing without an appointment but asked whether I might be able to see Bruce for a few minutes. The receptionist escorted me back to his office, where, as always, I was met with his signature greeting.

I said, "Bruce, I am not a suspect in Laura Smith's murder. In fact, a guy from Joplin has confessed and is being charged. I am here to move forward with the adoption."

"Will, all I need is your signature on a couple documents and we can get the process started." He sat down at his computer and began to print the documents.

"Do we have to declare what their last name will be at this point, or can we do that later? To my knowledge, James has never been told that he is my son. I need to have that conversation with him sooner rather than later."

"Will, they can keep their names and change them later, if they choose to at that time," Bruce said.

"I like that being an option. I would like that to be a decision they make, and they are still too young for that. I will discuss that with them today. Please file our case with them keeping the name Barro."

That evening, James, Little Jenni, and I walked along the creek and talked. I explained my conversation with Bruce earlier that afternoon. I think I was more concerned about breaking the news that James was my son and its impact on Little Jenni more than James. I described the letter Jenni had written to me but had not mailed.

"You mean my dad is not my dad?" James asked.

"That is not it really. Scott was the man who raised you until you were almost five years old. That makes him your dad. That will never change. What it means is that your mom believed I am also your dad," I explained.

He did not appear to be disturbed by the situation, but I watched him closely and told him I would be there to discuss it anytime if he had questions. As I expected, Little Jenni, with her sweet look of innocence, watched me with tears welling in her eyes and asked, "Does that mean you are not my dad?"

"That means your dad was and always will be Scott Barro. But if I adopt you, I hope I can become your father. That would mean the world to me," I said. "When the adoption is complete, you may keep your last name, Barro. When you are older, if you want your name to become Rogers, you can change it then. I think that is the best option for now. What do you think?"

James said, "As long as we stay with you, either way is fine."

Although I do not think she quite understood, Little Jenni studied me for a moment and nodded her agreement. I assumed James and I would discuss his issue in the future.

"How about if we build a bonfire and share stories about your mom? It has been a hard couple of weeks and it would be good to think of her and how much joy she gave us all. I really need that," I said.

It was with those words that I realized what they meant to me. All this time, I thought I was the one saving them.

Milton Keynes UK
Ingram Content Group UK Ltd.
UKHW021818010124
435297UK00016B/809